THE ART OF PIRACY

AN INSPECTOR DAVIDSON STEAMPUNK MYSTERY

CECILIA DOMINIC

ABOUT THE ART OF PIRACY

She unknowingly holds the secret to his immortality. When airship pirates attack, will their budding love go down in flames?

Alternate France, 1871. Art historian Veronica Devine dreams of putting her late husband's betrayal behind her, so she's grateful for the somewhat distracting mission to transport a valuable collection from a French chateau across the Atlantic. But before her voyage even begins, she's attacked by thieves and saved by a mysterious stranger.

Luc, the Marquis de Monceau's, fate is bound to an enchanted ancestral painting. After fleeing the Prussian invasion, his survival hinges on protecting an alias that preserves the rumor of his death. So when the beautiful woman he saves insists she has permission to remove his portraits, he has no choice but to escort her aboard a luxury airship.

Within the confines of the majestic vessel, Veronica and Luc soon discover they have more in common than a love of art. But cryptic messages, a clockwork automaton, and conniving passengers threaten to ground their romantic aspirations.

Will Veronica and Luc unravel the mystery of the masterpiece before dark forces from his past send their ship into the depths?

The Art of Piracy is the opening novella in the imaginative Inspector Davidson Mysteries steampunk romance series. If you like colorful characters, action-filled adventures, and intriguing settings, then you'll adore Cecilia Dominic's suspenseful drama.

1

———

Veronica Lillet Kindred shaded her eyes and looked up at the chateau. It appeared to be a typical opulent French manor, not one that deserved to have tales told about it of ghosts and strange occurrences. But the horses had gotten more nervous as they'd approached, and her crew quieter.

She didn't know any of the men that well, but they'd started the morning boisterous enough to the point of boasting that they'd capture the first spirit they encountered and put it in a glass jar. Then they'd bring it back to Paris and start doing séances, mediumship being a better paying profession than requisitioning and moving art.

The boasting had turned to nervous fidgeting and whispered repetition of rumors.

While Veronica had no doubt that men committed the sort of horrors that could produce specters, she didn't believe in ghosts. Still, something about the house felt...wrong. Like someone had taken the harmony of the place apart and put it back together with a note out of tune. Or something like that. She could never exactly describe the things she felt, only a sensation akin to the internal thrum at a concert when the instruments played loudly. Ironic since she'd only ever been passable at playing the pianoforte and singing, her first love being art. She'd learned during her time as an art history apprentice in London to pay attention when something stuck out as different. That's why Léonard Basquet, famous art historian and dealer, had sent her on this errand.

Focus, Veronica...

Even now her fingers twitched to sketch the archways and soaring lines of the chateau's windows and walls, but she quashed the feeling. Even if she had the time, she doubted the drawing would come. She hadn't been able to put pencil to paper and produce anything useful since Peter's death, and she doubted her once-prodigious talent would return now. Besides, there was no time for such frivolity. They had a shipment to assemble and an airship to catch.

"Allons-y," she said with as much authority as a young woman could command over a group of rough men. They muttered under their breath but complied, no doubt motivated by the bonuses they'd been promised. She pulled out her list and studied it. *Only about ten pieces*, she read for the hundredth time. *Enough to start a collection. I'll trust your good taste as to what to select. -Léonard*

A big responsibility. But hadn't she been waiting for the past four years for something like this? And it came along with the chance for her to return to Terminus in triumph, not as the disgraced girl who'd secretly married her headmaster and been widowed six months later.

The foreman took out an ornate key that looked like it came straight out of a fairy tale and applied it to the padlock on the large wooden front door. Although the rest of the chateau might boast modern upgrades, the Marquis had apparently decided to keep the old door, which was pitted and studded with iron. The squeak of its hinges lingered into a sigh that seemed to come from the depths of the house. With a shiver, Veronica wondered what sort of monster might emerge, but several seconds passed with no signs of life within.

No one wanted to go in first, so with a huff, Veronica led the way. A switch on the wall made gas lamps flare to life. So the Marquis *had* updated his property. Good. She hadn't relished the idea of using a torch or candle to illuminate the dark middle of a house filled with priceless objects. She feared setting something irreplaceable alight, or—the worst horror—burning the place down.

As the lights in the grand entrance hall flared to life, Veronica wondered if burning down the chateau would, indeed, be the worst horror. The place had obviously been evacuated quickly. Dust covered chairs that had been over-turned and iced moribund shapes on the floor that at first looked like animals but turned out to be scraps and articles of clothing. As Veronica and her crew followed the directions to the library, their movements kicked up the fine powder that swirled and eddied, making phantasmic shapes and casting faint shadows that tricked her peripheral vision. Underneath it all, the sigh that she'd heard when the door opened lingered and vibrated with its sense of wrongness.

Even so, she couldn't help a slight grin at the fact she led the way. The team of five burly men had fallen in behind *her*, and she congratulated herself on taking charge and showing courage.

See, Uncle Thaddeus, sometimes charging right in can be a good thing.

When they opened the double library doors and flipped the light switch, Veronica caught her breath. Two levels of books surrounded a large space anchored on the eastern wall by a fireplace, above which hung a large painting of Psyche and Eros in flight. The young god turned his face away, and Psyche gazed longingly at him. Veronica snorted. She knew that look. She'd *had* that look. Now she knew better.

"All right, down to business. Maurice and Gaston, you pack the crates. Lefoux and Armand, y'all, er, you follow me and bring the pieces I select to them. Carnais, stand guard." That last came out of her mouth almost involuntarily, and warmth crept into her face. Would they think her stupid or merely cautious? So far nothing had threatened them, at least not openly.

Carnais didn't argue, although someone muttered that muscle wouldn't protect them from whatever lurked in the chateau.

Veronica walked around the library on both levels and examined the paintings that hung between bookshelves, getting a sense of them. The Marquis' family had had eclectic tastes, although themes ran to the classical. She found a smaller Psyche and Eros, this of the young woman kneeling in front of piles of grain as the ants helped her sort them and Eros standing with his mother in the shadows in the background.

"This one." She indicated the painting. Although she found it annoying that Eros colluded with his mother in torturing his bride, she also felt a stab of satisfaction. Why not? That's what men did, wasn't it—hide things from their beloved that would tear things apart? Tear *them* apart?

She brought herself back to the moment with a shake of her head. There was no time for self-pity. That was all in the past. She had art to requisition.

Veronica chose several more, including a Flemish land-scape, a pre-Raphaelite languishing nymph, and what looked like a military tableau. Also a couple of small statues. Sadly they didn't have room or weight allowance for one of the gorgeous large kouros. The Archaic Greek statues' graceful white forms would have fit beautifully in a gallery. Too bad one of them appeared to be damaged. They had hinged limbs and could move, but thankfully they remained still. She didn't think her crew would have appreciated it if they had gone into their stereotypical motions.

She had room for one more picture and returned to one she'd been drawn to but couldn't see the obvious value of. An eight-by-twelve inch painting of a small boy sat in a frame on one of the center tables. It looked to have been painted at least a hundred years prior, but no artist's mark helped her place it or its worth. The child wore a blue ruffled suit and held a dimpled golden ball. When she picked it up, the energy around her increased in pitch and tone before falling into a hush. A noise from one of the upper galleries startled her, and one of the paintings she hadn't selected crashed to the floor, leaving an empty spot on the wall. Worse, there were two holes at eye distance about where the portrait's eyes would have been.

She shivered. Were they being watched?

The disturbance had spurred the men into action. One of them snatched the painting from her hands and put it in the crate with its fellow pieces. The crew murmured back and forth in French too fast for Veronica to catch, but she understood the meaning—they wanted to get out of there, and soon. She agreed. Whereas a phantasm or ghost would have been interesting, the thought of a person watching them? That was downright creepy.

Luc de Marcels, the late Marquis de Monceau, had not shuffled off the mortal coil in an airship accident, as was generally assumed. While he didn't mind the anonymity his presumed death had granted, he did resent having to lurk around his home like a ghost. Especially since it felt like something watched *him*.

At the moment, from the relatively hidden vantage point of

a painting's eyeholes, he observed a dreadfully composed young woman direct a group of ruffians to pack up *his* art in crates destined for who-knew-where. Paintings that had hung in the library for generations were being taken down and packed away like so much bric-a-brac. He would have stopped them but dared not be seen, for many reasons. There had already been one close call when the girl had examined the painting he hid behind, and he had almost not replaced the strip with the portrait's oil-painted eyes quickly enough.

The woman had taste, he'd give her that. She passed over paintings and statues he knew to be less valuable. Not that he had any sort of natural eye for art, but family lore had specified which works were to be taken if the chateau needed to be evacuated quickly. Admiration warred with irritation as he observed her. And while he was no longer a gambling man—his last wager had cost him an eye and his good looks—he bet one of the paintings that ended up in the straw-packed crates would be the one he sought.

He again cursed his father for not giving him specifics as to which painting would unlock the Monceau legacy, a legendary magical force originally harnessed by a wizard in the dark ages. He didn't need to sell any of the art. No, to do so would mark him as a thief and expose his true identity, which would lead to his being tried for treason.

They were almost finished, but she paused by one of the few pictures in standing frames, this one a painting of Luc's great grandfather as a boy. Or at least that's what he'd always been told. It had been painted by some no-name peasant artist and had little worth beyond family sentiment and history, but she lingered over it. What was she playing at? Did she truly not know what she sought?

Or, worse, did she? Could she know something, be more aware than he? It was possible, he conceded as he stepped back. He'd seen the artwork in the library so many times he'd ceased to *see* it. She looked at it for the first time, and he couldn't help but envy her.

A crash made him jump backward, and he guessed the portrait he'd been looking through had fallen. Icy sweat covered his skin. Something in the house wasn't happy about its desecration, and the sound of fluttering wings made him dash through the secret passages and down into the kitchen, behind which he'd tied his horse. He cursed at himself under his breath for his foolishness but didn't linger inside.

Those sounds and the constant feeling of being observed by something that had just awoken hungry had driven him from his home in the first place and on to that cursed airship. He suspected what he'd seen in the library indicated that Mademoiselle Art Thief would be departing France on a nice steamship. He'd have to follow her and find out.

His horse, Noir, made no sound as he approached. He'd trained the animal well, and together they quietly picked their way through the now-overgrown gardens. Seeing the estate's gradual decay made his heart hurt—his mother had been so proud of the grounds especially. He paused to watch the men load the crates into a carriage, and the crew arranged themselves, ready to depart. The young woman had just climbed on to the driver's bench beside the burly gentleman Luc had identified as the crew's foreman when a dark shadow painted the scene in shades of tar. He looked up to see the bulk of an airship descending, figures dressed in black dangling from ropes. Dark cloths covered the bottom halves of their faces, and each wore a black cap.

Now Luc cursed audibly and mounted his horse.

"Go, you fools!" he shouted at the woman and her crew, and they didn't hesitate. The carriage lurched forward, the man yelling at the horses to move their lazy rumps. The airship pursued them, and Luc calculated their odds. If the carriage made it down the drive across the lawn and into the Forêt de

Monceau, the trees would protect them. Luc only needed to keep the pirates from landing on the conveyance.

Luc held Noir's reins with one hand and urged his stallion forward. Noir obeyed, his burst of speed telling Luc the horse had been cooped up for too long. Luc unholstered his pistol, took quick aim, and shot at the pirate who was closest to the carriage. He prayed his shot would be high enough not to hit the carriage's drivers or occupants, and when the pirate fell, he knew his aim had been true. For once. He would deal later with the sickening certainty that if the bullet hadn't killed the man, the fall surely had.

Halfway to the forest, the carriage wobbled, and Luc sucked in a breath—would it lose a wheel? No time to worry about that problem. A bullet whizzed by his ear, and he urged Noir forward so they'd be under the airship and in its shadow, hopefully harder to target. He shot at the next closest pirate to the carriage and missed. That one fired back at him, but the motion of the airship made the ropes sway and twirl, and his bullet went wide. Still, Luc tried again.

Triumphant shouts brought his attention forward, and he saw the carriage disappear into the shadows of the trees. The pirates ascended their ropes, and Luc guessed—hoped—they'd given up. With one last burst of speed, Noir entered the forest, and its coolness enveloped them.

"And then he yelled, 'Go, you fools!' and shot at the pirates and kept them from capturing us." Veronica illustrated the scene with broad gestures, and Léonard grinned. Well, at least *he* found the situation amusing.

"And obviously, you did 'go,' fools that you were," he prompted.

Veronica took a deep breath to calm the thrumming of her

heart at the memory of the close call. Her eyes still stung when she thought about the wind and dust in them, and her fingers ached from clutching the side of the wagon, and then the reins, so tightly.

"It was harrowing," she admitted and took a sip of wine. "Utterly ha-arrowing." She didn't care if a slight Southern accent had crept into her words in spite of her effort to use overly proper English, as she'd been taught in London. It happened when she'd drunk too much wine or had become overly exhausted. Or when upset, like now.

How could her mentor just sit there and laugh and shake his head?

"So you made it to the forest, then? And back to Paris?" He sounded utterly delighted.

"With my eyes on the sky the entire time once we came out of the trees," she snapped. Finally, the pressure built in her chest to the point she had to exclaim, "At least you find this amusing! Do you know what it's like to have a ship full of pirates on your heels? In a rickety wagon with a barely competent driver? I had to take the reins from him or he'd've knocked us into a tree or overturned the stupid thing."

Gaston hadn't been pleased, and they'd spent the ride back to Paris in uncomfortable silence. None of the men would share their impressions with her in spite of her desire to give Léonard a complete accounting of the incident, so she had to fill in as many of the details as she remembered.

"Yes, as a matter of fact, I do." Léonard's expression snapped back to its customary somber demeanor when discussing serious matters, which for him typically consisted of alcohol or art. He ran the fingers of his right hand along his fashionably trimmed gray beard. "But the situation you describe is unusual."

"What do you make of it?" she asked. She'd often wondered about his past and how he, a man of upper years, had ended up teaching at King's College and collecting art in London. She knew it had something to do with the political unrest in France and him not being favored by the Emperor Napoleon III, hence why Léonard had finally been able to return. Napoleon III had been killed in the battle that ended the Prussian siege, and then the new government, after some turmoil, had taken over. But she'd never found out what Léonard had done to attract the emperor's dislike. Not that it mattered now. She'd come to find that the French nobles were easily insulted.

"It's rare for pirates to attack a house, but perhaps they were there for the same reason you were."

Veronica couldn't help a slight grin. "To requisition pieces of art to set up a new gallery in a city in the former Confederate States?"

"No, silly girl, and you know better. To loot the house. Perhaps they saw you and your crates and decided they wanted whatever you had."

Veronica sighed. "It seemed to be more than that. I can't tell you how I know..."

"You just do," he finished for her. During their five years of her working for him, he'd come to respect her intuition and her artistic eye, as he called it. It was why she'd moved from secretary to assistant to protégé. He leaned forward and put a hand on hers. "You know that if my old bones had been able to take the rough roads out to the estate, I would've been there."

She patted his hand with her free one, then brought both hands back to her lap. "I know, Léonard. It's just that..." She shrugged, unable to put all her feelings into words, so she settled on, "I thought this would be an easy assignment. Go to the disgraced, dead, and heirless noble's house, grab some art, and bring it back to Terminus."

She couldn't add, 'And show my family, especially my uncle, that I'm a capable, intelligent person who can make it on my own.' She'd never spoken of her family or her own disgrace to Léonard. She supposed they each had their own secrets.

"You know this may not be the last of it," Léonard said, and she looked up from her sole meunière.

"What? Why not?"

"Airship pirates roam all the oceans, including the Atlantic. You'll never see them—they're much too clever and good at using color, light, and shadow to their advantage. If there was something at the Monceau place they wanted, they won't stop until they get it."

Her intuition tickled the back of her brain. "What are you not telling me, Léonard?"

"Nothing, dear girl, nothing. I've given you all the information I have. It's up to you to do the rest. You proved yourself admirably today, especially after your driver was shot."

A sensation akin to electric shock made Veronica still. She hadn't mentioned that was why Gaston had been unable to control the horses—his left arm had been made immobile by a bullet to the shoulder, which he had only realized after the excitement and terror of the situation had passed. Thankfully the rest of the crew had all been veterans of the recent fighting and knew basic battlefield wound dressing and care, so he hadn't bled out. Or on the crates, and there was no danger of damage to their contents from seepage.

"More wine?" Léonard asked. "It sounds like you could use some to calm your nerves."

"Please," Veronica said and held out her glass. She forced herself to smile and pretend everything was all right, but she knew with certainty that Léonard held something back. And if it put her life in danger, that was one thing. If it imperiled her future triumph, well, she'd make sure that wouldn't happen.

At least he hadn't asked her to marry him again.

2

———

Luc threw the book he'd been leafing through for clues to the Legacy of Monceau against the wall, and it fell to the floor with a rustling thump. He buried his head in his hands and forced himself to take a deep breath. He should have realized he'd never be able to get anything done after the airship chase. He'd found the fallen pirate after the wagon had disappeared into the woods and the airship into the sky. The familiarity of the man's features confirmed for him what he had already suspected. La Belle Rouge had been the ship, and its captain likely behind the raid—or whatever it had been.

Why hadn't the pirates just landed in the yard and looted the house?

Because they sought the same thing he did. And they suspected the girl and her crew had it.

The creak of a floorboard made him wheel around, knife in hand. Not that it would do any good if someone held a gun on him, but at least he looked menacing. His former motto—"It doesn't matter how you feel, only how you look to others"—had come back to bite him in his French breeches in some disturbing ways, but he still had faith in the power of impressions.

"No harm, mate," Matthew Gelfman, physician to rogues and pirates, said, his hands up.

Luc lowered the knife. "Matt, what are you doing here? I'm surprised the captain let you off the ship."

"You know I'll go back." The man scrubbed a nervous hand over his thin stubbled cheeks. He wore no hat, and Luc could see that the little bits of hair he had left at his temples had gone gray. He'd also gotten thinner. "We all go back, Luc. That's how Rouge likes it. He doesn't take people hostage, he takes entire lives."

Luc placed the knife back in its sheath in his boot. "What does he want? I suppose he wasn't expecting for his men to encounter me this afternoon." He knew better than to play dumb. The captain of La Belle Rouge found out everything eventually. Legends had likened his attitude to the ruthlessness of Blackbeard. That was painting him nicely. As far as Luc could tell, the man had no soul. Not that he'd ever seen him—Captain Rouge, the man with no name and no face, only allowed a very trusted few access to him. But his commands were carried out with speed and precision.

"No, and he's not pleased." Matthew had only been allowed in to see the captain the previous year when Rouge had become ill and needed a physician. When he'd emerged and Luc had questioned him about the man who held them all captive, all Luc could get out of him was, "He's not what you'd expect." He refused to say more.

"What were they here for, then?" Luc pressed.

"They seek the same thing you do—the key to the fortunes of the Monceaus. Or Marcels. Or whatever your generation has chosen for its last name. Bloody confusing, if you ask me."

Luc didn't say why they chose a different surname every half-century or so. It was better to keep the populace guessing than have them notice the strange abilities of the Monceaus to stay young for a very, very long time.

But how had the pirates found out? He hadn't told anyone, had only hinted to Daphne. It was a conundrum, one of many he faced and didn't care for. Had he started talking in his sleep?

"So they weren't expecting anyone?" Luc asked.

"No, and when they saw the cart taking away what must'a been valuable stuff, maybe what they're looking for..." He shrugged.

Luc kept a neutral expression so as not to indicate he thought the pirates might be correct. He'd spent the afternoon searching for clues and had come up empty-handed. The young woman had taken the most likely possibilities with her. It made sense that his forbears had commissioned decoy art— like the one he'd brought with him originally. He still mentally smacked himself on the head for being fooled like he'd been.

"You didn't have to interfere, Luc." Matthew walked over to him but didn't touch him. Instead, he folded his arms as though he'd suddenly walked into a draught or could feel Luc's chill toward him. "And now one of the mates is dead, and Rouge is pissed. They told Rouge how you picked him off his rope from a moving horse. Impressive."

"It was a lucky shot. I haven't had good aim since..." He gestured to the eyepatch that hid his missing eye. But he knew he and Matthew danced around the inevitable. "What does he want?"

"He's adding to Madame Cinsault's ransom. Good, *loyal* pirates are hard to find."

Luc didn't miss the stress on loyal. "I never signed up to join him even though I may look the part."

"But you're an asset. And you got him curious with your quick healing."

"Not quick enough," Luc growled. Every day he checked to see if, by some miracle, his eye had grown back. And every day's look in the mirror horrified and disappointed him. Could the Monceau legacy regenerate an eye? Only time would tell. "How much to the ransom?"

Matthew named a number that made Luc, typically a shrewd gambler, raise his eyebrows.

"That's impossible."

Matthew shrugged. "But it's what he wants." He lowered his voice even though they were alone. Or were they? A rustling noise made Luc's blood temperature drop. "You know he's not going to release you until you part with your legacy. Or at least share the secret of it."

"A man who refuses to be seen or spoken to can't condemn others for their secrets," Luc muttered, but he knew Matthew's words to be true. Rouge would never release him.

"Follow the girl," Matthew urged. "Figure out where the paintings went and which one you need. Then you'll at least have the bargaining chip."

Luc didn't say he was planning to do just that, but not necessarily to bargain with Rouge. While he wanted to rescue Daphne Cinsault from the pirate's ship, he suspected there would be no rescue or way to meet Rouge's demands. He'd try once more to have her released, but then he'd disappear.

And isn't part of this because you're tired of her? a little voice at the back of his head asked. *You've never stayed with one woman for so long. Familiarity and contempt, you know.*

Luc brushed the words away, or tried to. Even if Daphne Cinsault were to mean something to him, she'd become too much of a liability. For one thing, the only way Rouge could have found out about the Monceau legacy and what it potentially meant could have been if Daphne had told him. At least, that's what he surmised. The entire thing became convoluted with too much thought.

He missed the days when complicated meant having to choose what three cheeses to serve with wine after dinner.

"Fine," Luc spat. "I'll follow her out of Paris, wherever she goes."

"Good. You know Rouge will be watching for you. You can't go far."

Luc nodded, resigned.

Matthew turned and melted into the shadows. Luc didn't follow him. He didn't feel like it. He'd give the library one more sweep and then be on his way.

As for the girl, he hoped she'd at least be grateful that he'd saved her life. She had more trouble than she could handle heading for her.

The shadows at the end of the hallway thickened, and he stepped back, the sickening memory of his last night at the chateau sweeping through his mind. Like last time, he couldn't move, couldn't speak. But then he'd been asleep, and now he was wide awake.

"Monceau," the voice said from the shadows. Not a voice, exactly. More a loud, rasping sigh, as though it gathered the sounds from around it and concentrated them into something not quite human.

"What do you want?" Luc asked.

"Restore your legacy." Two glowing eyes appeared, and the shadows coalesced into the dark shape of a man in eighteenth-century dress. If Luc had been looking at a mirror, he would have first thought it was him, but indeed, it was more of a doppelganger. With two eyes, lucky bastard.

"I'm trying to, Grandfather."

The shadows pointed a thin finger at him. "You've lost too much. Do not lose this."

Rustling noises filled Luc's ears. He'd originally thought they came from the painting of Psyche and Eros, but no, they surrounded him, and he recognized them as the clothing of centuries gone by. Sweeping skirts, dragging capes, and whispers. So many whispers.

There had always been rumors that the Monceau heirs had something strange about them, something special, especially since they disappeared every so often abroad, and a new one came back in his place. The new Monceau had a variant of the last name and looked enough like the previous ones that there was no question they were related. But the whispers never died.

In truth, there had only ever been four Marquis de Monceaux, and the last one had died in the seventeenth century.

As his ancestors chased him down the hall, into the kitchen, and out into the back courtyard, where he had to calm a frightened Noir, Luc wondered for the hundredth time what price his first ancestor, a follower of the neo-Pythagoreans, had paid for their almost-immortality.

VERONICA SQUINTED up at the overly bright cream-colored balloon of the *Acadia Pearl*. At least that's how it seemed under the cloudless blue sky with the sun at its most cheerful—and annoying—angle. The luxury airship, the first of its kind to promise "Southern Charm with European Class for your Transatlantic Flights to the Former Confederacy," strained against the ropes holding it to the ground as though eager to be off. Although Veronica had been looking forward to joining the inaugural flight, the unease that had crept upon her during her conversation with Léonard had overtaken her excitement. So had all the wine, leaving her this morning with a dull headache and a dry mouth that no amount of tea or water could fix.

She'd expected Léonard's revelation to throw everything topsy-turvy, and she'd spent the morning looking out for...well, she didn't know what. But events had run smoothly. The crates with the paintings had been delivered to the airship from their storage locker at the hotel, and now a fussy little customs agent looked them over and filled out a bill of lading for her to show to the American—not Confederate, she reminded herself—agent on the other end.

"And where did you say these came from?" he asked, looking at her over his round, wire-framed lenses. His nose twitched like a rabbit's, making the ridiculous mustache underneath wiggle absurdly. She wondered if he had some sort of extra ability to sniff out hidden valuables that someone might try to sneak in or out of France.

"The Chateau de Monceau," she patiently explained for the third time. "With the permission of Stephan de Moray, Minister of Artistic Objects." She'd never heard of such a position before coming to France, but she'd surmised that the French government had a ridiculous number of minor ministries. It was like a spider whose legs would keep wiggling even if the head were smashed.

"And they're headed for a gallery in Terminus," he clarified —again—and made a notation on the form.

"Yes. The new city gallery."

"*Bien*. It is good for you to expose the barbaric Southerners to the beauty of art."

Veronica bit her tongue. While she hadn't supported the Confederacy—and indeed had escaped to Europe because her family didn't—she bristled at being called *barbaric*. But she'd dealt with such men before and simply forced her lips to lift in what she hoped passed for a pleasant smile.

A gong sounded on board the airship, and Veronica checked her pocket watch—twenty minutes to departure.

"I don't mean to rush you, Monsieur," she said, "but that was the first departure bell."

"Ah, yes, just one more minute." He adjusted his glasses and dug around in the crate. The breeze picked up wisps of straw and blew them around Veronica in a mini cyclone. She batted them away with one hand while holding on to her parasol with the other so it, too, wouldn't take off.

"Is there a problem?" A dark shadow fell over the crate, and the customs agent squinted up.

Veronica turned to give the newcomer a sharp warning to step away—he'd only delay things further—but caught her tongue. The man was well-dressed with a mop of dark brown hair and tanned skin. A jagged scar over his left cheekbone ended at an eyepatch. Which was a pity, she thought, because he must have been beautiful before the injury had destroyed his facial symmetry and flint-black eye. Now he simply looked dangerous. And, she had to admit, interesting, with an air of authority.

"No, no, monsieur," the agent squeaked. "I am just finishing up. Madame, would you like me to close the crates?"

Another gong—fifteen minutes to departure.

"No, just lay the lids across them. I'll have the porters nail them shut." She didn't think the fastidious little man would agree, but he nodded, signed the bill of lading, and shoved it at her before scampering off.

"Customs agents can be such a bore," the stranger said in accented English, the corner of his mouth on the uninjured side of his face lifting in a half-grin. "I believe they no longer hear the departure gongs. You wouldn't have been the first to have missed your ship because of their fastidious incompetence."

"I... Thank you." She returned the faint smile. "And I like that expression—fastidious incompetence."

"It's a curse of our government, I'm afraid." He held out an arm. "May I escort you?"

Veronica bit back a refusal. She was heading back to Terminus, after all, and would lose the freedom to move about that being a widow had granted her in Europe. Well, a widow who appeared harmless and uninterested in any further marriage prospects. She might as well get used to needing an escort, although she did not intend to follow that custom while in flight.

"Yes, thank you."

He signaled to a group of porters, who rested the lids on the crates and carried them aboard the airship.

Once there, the stranger said, "I trust you can take it from here."

"Yes, thank you." She appreciated his not lingering.

He tipped his top hat and bowed, and then departed. She'd noticed his biceps muscles tighten as they walked up the plank to the gondola and wondered what his reaction had meant. Did he not like flying? Was he prone to airsickness?

"Madame," the lead porter said, "may we bring these to the storage hold?"

"Let me check them first." Again. She'd confirmed the contents several times since that morning, but she couldn't shake the fear that something would disappear, and she'd be blamed as she had been as a child when one of her cousins had lost a toy or ribbon or other possession that wasn't valuable until it had gone missing.

She checked through the straw and confirmed that everything was there. The painting of the child with the ball looked up at her, and she plucked it out of the straw.

"I'll take this one," she said. "He'll keep me company in my room."

The porter made a note on the cargo manifest sheet, had her sign it, and then they nailed the crates shut and whisked them away. Well, with as much whisking as four men carrying heavy crates between them could manage. At least she knew her art was aboard.

And now she had an interesting new mystery—the man who had rescued her from the customs agent. The intriguing gentleman looked like a laborer but had the air and sophistication of a noble. She wondered if she'd see him again. And if she'd feel a certain warmth in her core if she had the chance to touch him again?

Don't be a fool, Veronica. Your family won't take you seriously if you come home with a Frenchman on your arm. But at the moment, her family seemed very far away.

Henry Davidson, typically known as Inspector Davidson but now simply referred to as "Monsieur Henry" by the airship crew, watched the passengers board. A tap on his shoulder made him turn to see a young man in uniform.

"The captain would like a word, Sir."

Henry followed the youth to the captain's office.

"How has your time in Paris been?" Captain Viero asked once they'd exchanged the usual introductory pleasantries.

"Relaxing," Henry lied. While he'd enjoyed strolling the Champs Elysees and visiting the landmarks, he'd not been able to escape a sense of restlessness and unease. He should have been grateful that his life's work—seeking out and uncovering the plots of the neo-Pythagoreans and Clockwork Guild—had been justified by the appearance of a goddess at a Boston businessman's party. If not a goddess, then some supernatural force. But whenever he closed his eyes, he relived the scene where he'd made his biggest mistake—allowing a powerful Clockwork Guild member to escape since it had been part of a bargain he'd made for another man's freedom. He had thought through the scenario so many times it had become etched on his brain, but he couldn't figure a way out. Or how he could have done anything differently.

Thus his superiors, deciding his error indicated he needed a vacation, had sent him to Europe, which, as he bitterly conceded, was far away from the site of the strange occurrences. And he agreed he needed a vacation. His left leg, which had been injured, throbbed when it was about to rain, and so his walking had been not so much for touring as for strengthening.

Now he sat across from Captain Viero, a tall Italian man with a dramatic mustache, and accepted a brandy.

"I was wondering if you could do me a favor," Viero said. "I have heard rumors of airship pirates over the Atlantic."

"As have I," Henry said. "But it's a big ocean."

"Yes, but the word is that they attack at the behest of someone 'on the inside' as you English speaking persons like to say."

"Ah." Henry nodded, the certainty of what he was about to be asked to do sinking in. "So you want me to keep an eye out for anything suspicious."

Viero nodded. "That is precisely what I am asking. As a thank you, the cost of your voyage will be refunded. To you." He raised his eyebrows, and Henry got the hint—he'd get the money in cash, and his superiors wouldn't be any the wiser.

Had the offer been made to him before the events of the previous spring, he would have thrown it back in the captain's face, his integrity and keeping things above-board the most important things to him. But now that they had dismissed him, sent him overseas instead of allowing him to clean up his mess... Perhaps he could use the money. At any rate, he would decide later whether to return it to them.

He shifted. He'd made his decision, but he still didn't feel right about it. "What, precisely, do you want me to do?"

"Talk to the other guests and passengers. Mingle with them. Use that famous sense of yours to see whether anything suspicious is occurring."

Henry scoffed. "What famous sense?"

"Those of us in the Airship Corps, regardless of country,

have heard of The English Fox." Piero tapped his nose. "I can only assume that is you."

Henry wanted to be flattered by the nickname but instead chastised himself for not being more careful. "I cannot confirm that the nickname applies to me, Viero. And really, who came up with that ridiculous moniker?"

"I believe it was an American Lieutenant by the name of Davinia Crow."

Henry had to call upon every ounce of espionage training he'd had to not react to the woman's name. She'd had the audacity to kiss him. And, damn himself, he'd had the weakness to like it. He hoped that the heat he felt in his cheeks and crawling up his neck would be attributed to the warmth of the cabin, its wide windows bathed in streaming sunlight.

Viero smirked. Well, so much for that, Henry thought. Thankfully, the captain didn't press the matter.

"So you will agree to help me?" he asked.

Henry had to admit he'd been dreading the boredom of the voyage in spite of it being an amazing, modern vessel equipped with every comfort. This could add some interest to his journey. Who knew what he'd find?

"I will help you," Henry said. "Although I'm not sure what I can do if a pirate attack is an inside job, as you said. I would imagine that they're good at hiding out."

An unfamiliar gravity descended upon Viero. "You need to realize what we lose if you fail." He stood and gestured for Henry to follow him.

"Stand here," Viero said and fitted a small golden key into a barely perceptible hole on the side of his desk. A trap door opened at Henry's feet. He followed Viero down the ladder into the darkness.

Once at the bottom, Viero lit a phosphorus lamp and shone it around them. They stood in a hidden hangar under the captain's office. A small sleek metal ship with wings stood in front of them. It looked to Henry like it crouched, ready to spring to life at a touch.

"What is it?" Henry asked.

"The next generation of airship," Viero told him. "An experimental prototype. And a secret gift from France to the United States. It was the emperor's wish that it should be given to them upon achieving their peace."

"Does it fly?"

Viero shrugged. "I do not know. I've not tried. I can't tell you how it works, only that an engine causes it to make its own breeze, which then lifts the wings." He gestured for Henry to precede him up the ladder.

"Now," Viero said once they sat across from each other at his desk again. "You see why I need your help."

Henry nodded. He only hoped he'd manage to not mess this assignment up, too.

3

After leaving the beautiful—well, interesting-looking, at least—art thief, Luc made himself walk about the airship. The gondola had three levels, all comprised of different areas and rooms depending on class. Whereas those in first-class had free rein of the entire vehicle except for the crew's quarters, technical areas, and storage, the other passengers were limited to their decks. His contact had gotten him a first-class ticket, which Luc could hardly afford considering his rapidly dwindling stash. He'd picked up a few more coins at the chateau, but the ghosts had chased him out before he could get too many. They'd made their displeasure and disappointment at him allowing art to leave the chateau known. But why hadn't they spooked the woman and her crew?

He knew the answer before his mind had asked the question—because he'd been there, so the spirits thought he was allowing the theft. Ghosts, he'd come to realize, were dashedly difficult to reason with.

So now he was aboard another accursed airship trying to get his air legs under him so he didn't stumble about like a drunken fool as he had on the pirate ship. There he'd had Daphne to help him. Here he had no one, and the recognition of his isolation descended upon him, a dark cloud of ennui and resignation. How many times in his past had he been trapped in the same dark place? How many times had he turned to women, wine, or gambling so he could feel something again?

There were many periods to recall during his long life. Was that the Monceau curse, the mirror to the legacy—the moods that overtook him when he least wanted them?

He shook his head. The way he felt currently didn't match his previous experience of what he'd come to recognize as The Monceau Mood. No, he simply hated airships, and he couldn't afford to give up yet another eye when things went belly up, as part of him knew they would. He needed to search the woman's crates, find the art that would lead him to the legacy, and spirit it away without her knowing. He had just enough money for passage back to France once he did.

He passed by a window and caught a glimpse of his reflection. His horrid visage scowled back at him, and he forced his expression into more neutral territory. The girl—woman, he amended, since having been close to her he'd realized her age was closer to twenty-five than the late teens his original impression had been—wouldn't trust him if he scowled like a monster. A grumpy beast, he called himself, and then laughed before reining that reaction in. If someone saw him, they'd think he was insane, laughing to himself, although he often did so in private at the irony of life.

His perambulations brought him from the first-class deck to the second-class level, which was darker, more crowded, and full of cigar smoke from the men sitting around and playing cards. Many of them glanced at him, then away, and he bristled at the dismissal. He knew he no longer belonged with the nobility and nouveau riche of the upper deck. But these individuals didn't have the right to reject him. He found a table with an open chair and sat. The other three men looked at him in surprise.

"What do you want, Monsieur?" the man across from him asked. His thinning dark hair seemed to be migrating down to his jowls, which sported gray-flecked muttonchop sideburns.

"To play cards, of course," Luc said, making his expression as pleasant as possible.

The man to his right, who had sandy brown hair and a thin face, shook his head. "Your game's going to be too rich for the likes of us, gov'nor."

"Ah, an Englishman," Luc said and smiled. "How would you know? I am but a poor man like the rest of you."

"Them's on the lower deck," the third man growled. His cigar smoke wreathed him so thickly that Luc could barely make out an aquiline nose and gray hair, but the one glimpse was enough. It was Monsieur Firmin, former director of the L'Ecole d'Archaeologie. Luc wanted to ask him if he was gambling away the money he'd stolen from his students, tuition collected before telling them the school was closing, but thought better of it. The man's affecting a rough English accent told Luc he wanted to remain anonymous, and Luc filed that fact away for future reference. And use.

"My apologies, then," Luc said and rose. He didn't want to risk Firmin recognizing him as well. Not that he would with the eyepatch, the scar, and the stone and a half weight loss since Luc hadn't been able to eat normally for several weeks after his injury. Luc wondered if his own mother would have known him, poor woman. She'd died of consumption when he'd been a twenty-something year-old young man who still looked like an early teenager. His father had been debating telling her the secret of the Monceaus, but she'd gone to the next world before he could. Or maybe he had, and she'd died of shock. Luc had never found out.

He wandered through second-class to the lounge, which

looked bare compared to the opulence of the first-class one above.

"Pirate!" a young voice piped up, and the entire area stilled. He felt the weight of a hundred gazes upon him.

"Hush," a woman said, clamping her hand over a young boy's mouth. "Apologies, Monsieur."

"No offense taken," Luc said, the dark mood hovering just above him. At least the child hadn't called him a monster. He climbed back up to the airy, well-lit first-class floor and took a seat in the lounge across from a man reading a newspaper.

"So what brings you aboard?" the man asked in an English accent and lowered the paper.

Blast it all, of all the rotten luck... Luc smiled, leaned back, and tried to decide how to answer Inspector Henry Davidson, the man who had ferreted out neo-Pythagoreans across the globe and who had been getting uncomfortably close to Luc—and his secrets—for several years.

VERONICA SET her reticule on the little nightstand in her room and looked around. Although she'd booked a first-class berth, everything was small, with barely enough room for her to turn around in her skirt, and she barely wore a bustle. The bed sat under the window with the nightstand between it and the door to the water closet, which held a shower, sink, and toilet. She admired the modern touch of the shower but wondered how she'd manage to fit in there, skirts and all, to take care of other business. Ah, well, she'd figure it out. Women always did.

There was a little writing desk that folded down from the wall opposite the bed, presumably so one could sit upon the bed and do one's correspondence. Not that there would be any way to mail anything beyond the limited supply of carrier pigeons, both real for shorter journeys and clockwork for longer ones. She doubted she would be high enough on the hierarchy to rate the ability to send anything by pigeon. Consequently, she'd posted everything before she left, the urgent letters such as those to her family telling them of her imminent arrival by mail airship, the rest by steamer.

She pulled out the letter she'd received from Peter's mother, who lived in Charleston, the day before. It had been waiting for her at her hotel when she'd returned from the Chateau Monceau.

My dear child,

I hope this letter finds you well. I asked your aunt where I should send correspondence, and she directed me to send this to a hotel in Paris, as you are no longer in London. How delightful for you! I often wished I could be a woman of the world, traveling to the great cities to see the sights. But I do not regret staying in Charleston and raising my family. Peter was the joy of my life and heart, and I still miss him every day.

Veronica snorted at that. Had Mrs. Kindred known what a liar her son had been? Still, Veronica couldn't help but read on.

I am hoping that when the Acadia Pearl *lands in Charleston, you'll take a few hours to come say hello to your grieving mother-in-law. I have a house on the Battery, and I am fortunate it was only minimally damaged in the shelling we endured for those long years. Perhaps I can show you around, share places with you that Peter loved. I am aware you were his student, so perhaps he's already told you about his past. But still, although he is gone, I do want to get to know you better. If I had known that his last trip home would end with him mortally ill, I would have done anything I could to have prevented it, and I'm sure you tried. I can only imagine your sorrow, having been married such a short time before you had to let him go. Ah, well, he was always such a strong-willed person; he would not have let either of us dissuade him, I am sure.*

ANOTHER SNORT. Veronica noted to herself she really ought to stop that—she'd sound like the barbaric Confederate pig others accused Southerners of being. But no, nothing would have dissuaded Peter from following his duty when he was drafted.

IF YOUR AIRSHIP departs on time—and how often do they? But with it being the inaugural voyage, I'm sure they'll do their best to be punctual—you will likely not have time to send a reply. Therefore, I will hope to receive you at my home at three o'clock on Tuesday, July 11.
With love,
Teresa Kindred

"HOW COULD YOU LOVE ME? You don't even know me," Veronica asked the letter, aware she sounded like a fool talking to herself. But what could the woman want? Veronica couldn't imagine having any sort of a relationship with someone she'd never met. Did Teresa Kindred know her son had liked to keep secrets? That he'd loved to arrange events and people around him to suit his ideas of what life should be like? She'd been so stupid, so young and impressionable to have allowed herself to be duped like she had. She'd given him everything, her soul, body, and art, and she would never have found out the truth had he lived. Living men don't make deathbed confessions. And then what would have happened? She would have stayed as the wife of the headmaster of a boarding school, a finishing school for spoiled girls whose families wanted to educate them so they'd be better marriage prospects. Or teachers, as Veronica's uncle had envisioned for her. He'd recognized her independent streak, at least, but still had not allowed for her own ambitions.

The takeoff gong resonated through the airship. A gentle pressure on the soles of her shoes and a dizzying shift in her peripheral vision told her the airship had lifted off. She kneeled on the bed and looked out of the window, watching Paris grow smaller and smaller until it became a dark smudge at the edge of a patchwork of green fields, including the airship field they'd just departed from. She wondered if the little customs agent had watched the massive dirigible take off or if he'd had his rabbity nose buried in a ledger somewhere, regretting not having looked at her shipment more carefully. She'd been honest and accounted for everything.

The airship hit a rough patch of air, and she clutched the windowsill as the vehicle shook, then returned to its smooth sense of gliding. If she closed her eyes, she could hear and feel the hum of the engines that permeated the entire vessel.

A small crash made her open her eyes, and she looked down to see the painting of the boy with the ball had fallen off the nightstand, where she thought she'd placed it carefully. Perhaps the liftoff, then turbulence had caused it to shift, but she'd braced it against the wall behind her reticule, so she didn't know how it could have made its way forward and to the floor. Thankfully it didn't seem to be damaged.

She picked it up and sat with her back against the wall, her feet on the floor in case of more turbulence. It made for an awkward half-sideways position, but she could at least examine the picture in full sunlight in a way she couldn't in the gloom of the chateau. She wondered what it had looked like on the night of the final ball, which she'd read about in old newspapers. Something strange had happened, and first one of the musicians had fled with two guests, and then other attendees had departed in a rush as well. It was like something had been awakened, one breathless reporter had said. Even the Marquis had come back to the city and been trapped there during the Prussian siege. Then he'd died in an airship accident trying to escape.

"Is that what happened?" she asked the boy in the picture. "The end of your line? It feels like your story isn't over." Indeed, she could normally sense finality, just as she could sense things of great value. But this was different. It was more like the path changed, not that it had ended, although she couldn't have explained what she meant if anyone had pressed her. That particular talent had helped her to advise Léonard on what paintings were, indeed, a master's final work. And which artworks indicated that more pieces had followed, even if they hadn't been discovered yet.

In the sunlight, the marks on the ball, which had looked like dimples, came alive as dim symbols. The picture had a layer of grime on top of it, and she wondered if she could find appropriate cleaning agents for it. If she could, it might lead to an interesting discovery, although, again, she didn't know what.

But a tingling sensation raced from her neck to her lower back and down her arms. She knew the painting hid something important, and she aimed to find out what.

She placed it carefully on the nightstand again, this time with her reticule holding it more firmly in place, and rose. She left the room, locking the door behind her and putting the loop of string that held her key around her wrist so she wouldn't lose it. She had a trunk tucked under the bed that contained some skirts with pockets, but she'd worn her nicer one so as to appear...what? Suitable for air travel? Like a lady?

That didn't matter now. She was on the hunt. Time to find a crewman to direct her to the cleaning supply closet.

WHEN THE MAN in the eyepatch sat across from him, Henry wondered if it was possible for the pirate's accomplice aboard the ship—if, indeed, there was one—to be so obvious. The man looked like he'd spent a great deal of time outside. His skin showed the ruddiness of sun exposure with a lighter line along his scalp where a hat would have presumably kept the sun off his face. His scar was also darker than the rest of his face, not lighter, indicating its recency and sun exposure. And the fact it ended in an eyepatch...

No, that couldn't be him. Still, it wouldn't hurt to check.

"Good afternoon, Monsieur," Henry said in French and lowered his paper.

Surprise flickered over the man's face to be replaced by a look of recognition, then that was swept away by a cautious scowl. Still, he said in accented English, "And to you, sir."

"Ah, it's that obvious I'm an Englishman, then?" Henry asked with what he hoped was a disarming grin. He'd never been good at the introductory small talk, always preferring to go in for the kill—or intelligence, as the case may be—sooner rather than later. But it was still a dance, and he could pretend to enjoy it.

"Your accent is distinct, although your pronunciation isn't bad," the man admitted. He hadn't relaxed into his chair, but rather sat forward, his elbows on his knees.

"What brings you to this lovely ship?" Henry asked, staying with English since it seemed as though the other man preferred to converse with him in it. Goodness, was his French accent that atrocious? "Pleasure voyage?"

"More a voyage of necessity." He stood. "Good day."

"Wait," Henry said and also stood. The man arched an eyebrow, and the gesture led to a sense of recognition that almost knocked Henry back into his chair. He went through some mental adjustments. *Take away the scarred half of the face, replace it with the unscathed part, and make the hair longer and tied back... Then add twenty pounds and foppish clothing rather than the dark browns and blacks of the man's current attire, and it could be the Marquis de Monceau.*

But no, the Marquis had died in an airship accident. Edward Bailey and Patrick O'Connell, two reliable witnesses, had seen the vessel blow up in mid-air. O'Connell had sent Edward back to the Théâtre Bohème and helped with the debris, including human remains. But he'd said something about the body parts being unidentifiable. So, it was possible.

Henry recognized he stared, and he'd been silent for a socially awkward long time.

"You... remind me of someone," Henry said. "I'm sorry. It's been a long day already. Please, what is your name?"

The man hesitated, then held out a hand. "Stephan Cloutier, art dealer, at your service."

Henry shook his hand, now more intrigued. The Marquis had been known for his eclectic tastes and art collection. And wild parties that had suddenly ceased due to strange occurrences at the Chateau Monceau.

"And so you're traveling to the Confederate States for...?"

Cloutier drew his hand back. "I believe it is customary upon introduction to offer one's own name upon introduction, Sir."

Henry noted the slip. "I'm Henry Davidson. Simply on vacation. Haven't ever seen the Southern states, so I'm curious now that they're at peace and open again." The lies slipped smoothly past his teeth, and he hated how easily he could deceive. So what if Cloutier was Monceau? They all had their secrets. And if the Marquis had somehow managed to make it away from the airship accident and sported injuries as a result, then he had every right to his privacy. Henry had been informed of the treason charges and the price on Luc de Moncels, who'd not been stripped of his title but still remained in disgrace.

Cloutier pressed his lips together and nodded. "Good day to you, Monsieur. I hope your voyage is comfortable."

He turned to leave, but a scream split the cabin's peace.

4

————

Veronica left her room, excited for the chance to have her own private art project. Sure, she had plenty of paperwork to do, cataloging the pieces she'd collected and filling out notes based on what she'd learned about the Marquis de Monceau during her time in Paris. Léonard had introduced her to some mutual acquaintances of his and Monceau's, including Monsieur Firmin, former director of the L'Ecole d'Archaeologie, which had been based out of the Louvre until the Prussian Siege had closed the school and scattered the students. Léonard had later confided in Veronica that Firmin would likely be fleeing Paris, as the authorities had connected him to the disappearance of the students' tuition deposits for the Spring 1871 semester. However, when she'd met Firmin, he'd seemed stern and not the type to do something like steal a bunch of young men and women's money. But then, she'd not proven to be a great judge of character.

The Marquis, from what she'd heard of him, had not been a gentleman. His love of wine, women, and art was legendary. Léonard had told her after she'd returned to Paris with her finds, as they'd stood over them, that there was a story of how the Marquis would bring young women into the library and not tell them that some of the kouros statues had moving parts. Then, when they fainted, he would catch them in his arms, or if they became frightened, grab them by the hand and run with them into a private alcove, where things that a proper young woman shouldn't know about happened. Veronica had reminded Léonard that she'd been married and had some experience, but he only smiled and shook his head.

"You're still an innocent, Madame, even if you've worn a wedding band in your past."

She didn't tell him that she and Peter had engaged in premarital activities while she was still a student and he her headmaster. She didn't want to give Léonard, who became uncomfortably affectionate after a few glasses of wine, any ideas.

So the Marquis had been a cad. She wasn't surprised. Many men, especially those in power, were, and they liked to take advantage of women. Her own uncle had certainly seemed to enjoy exercising power over her, even to the point of dictating her future. And telling her she had no talent for drawing, allowing that large part of her soul to wither until she had gone off to school and found it again under a cherry tree with a sparrow who'd begged her to draw his portrait. Or at least that's what she'd thought.

She touched the pin she wore on her breast, a miniature golden bird who reminded her of her sparrow. Even though she'd lost her ability to draw, she could at least remember the joy it had given her. And she could do her best to restore old or damaged art to ensure others appreciated it.

She emerged onto the main deck lounge, where groups of wicker chairs with cushions surrounded low tables, some of which held tea or other beverages in grooved trays. She stopped and took in the colors—the deep blue of the sky as the backdrop, the light tan of the furniture, the bright red of the cushions, and the sober hues of the clothing the men and women wore. In these post-war times, people tended to save color for frivolous occasions like balls and parties. During the day, the colors people wore and emotions they showed were muted by the knowledge they all had to keep foremost in mind—there had been wars. Very bad things had happened. They must mourn and not forget.

If there was one thing Veronica had learned from her study of art and the history that made it, it was that men never learned. There would always be wars for stupid reasons. Or noble ones, as in the case of the War Between the States to free the enslaved people in the South. For all she hated her uncle, she admired him for not having bowed to the pressure to have enslaved servants, although he'd made liberal use of indentured ones and had not always treated them well. She hadn't liked his attitude toward them, especially as it became clear that her place in the household sat just barely above theirs, and when she was asked to help out when they were short-handed, she couldn't say no. Her cousins Lucy and Daisy never had to do anything besides what was expected of them as good Southern ladies.

She shook her head to clear it of the resentment that hovered just out of awareness. Lucy and Daisy weren't here on an inaugural voyage of a luxury airship floating over the Atlantic. They hadn't traveled all over Europe and hadn't been in and out of noble houses looking at amazing things. And— she caught sight of her pirate, as she'd started thinking of him —they hadn't been rescued from fastidious government officials by dashing men in eyepatches.

Veronica started to walk toward where he sat, drawn there by some unseen force she couldn't name. She only wanted to thank him again, that's all. There was no reason for her to speak to him otherwise. Why, they hadn't been properly introduced.

But did it matter up here? She'd noticed on the steamship that brought her to Europe that once land disappeared, so did some social morays and morals, and the boundaries between couples had loosened. She hadn't partaken in any scandalous behavior—hadn't wanted to—and had the perfect excuse with her widow's veil and black dress and gloves. While she mourned the idea of what she'd thought she and Peter had had rather than the man himself, her heart was still broken over the whole affair.

The pirate stood, as did the man he'd been talking to, and Veronica could see from the tightening of the rogue's jaw that he wasn't pleased. He glanced her way, and she ducked behind a plant, not willing for his angry gaze to fall on her. She didn't want him to see her watching him or to associate her with whatever conspired between him and the thin man opposite him. Veronica couldn't see his face, only his reddish-brown hair, cropped close in the style of a lawman's, and she noticed that he wore a tweed jacket like a university professor. Her curiosity got the better of her, and she made her way toward them, straining to hear what they said.

"I believe it is customary for a man to offer his own name upon introduction, Sir," the pirate said, his voice smooth and deadly.

Veronica paused. Drat, she'd missed his name. Fine, she'd have to get him to give it to her.

She had almost screwed up the nerve to approach them when a woman's scream made her wheel around and knock into a waiter, who dropped a tray with a tea service. The porcelain shattered and the brown liquid splattered and dripped across the striped carpet.

"Stupid, clumsy girl," the voice of memory said. Her face

burning in shame, Veronica bent to help the waiter clear the debris, but he batted her hands away.

"Don't hurt yourself, Mademoiselle. Thank you for bumping me," he said in heavily accented English with a wink of one dark blue eye. "I would have likely dropped it anyway, and you gave me an, ah, excuse."

"I'm dreadfully sorry," she said. "The scream startled me, too. Oh, dear," she said and stood, wiping her hands on her skirts. "I hope no one is hurt." She turned to see the pirate and the man he'd been talking to glance her way, then head toward the door that led to the stairs down to the second-class deck.

"Only my pride," the waiter said, straightening. His white jacket was stained brown with the tea, and the tray he held was full of shards. He looked down and grimaced.

"I'm truly sorry," she said, although she knew that repeating the apology wouldn't remedy the situation. She'd always been so clumsy! It was a wonder she'd ever been able to muster enough coordination to hold a pencil, much less draw.

And of course those thoughts would surface, and her mind would plan the lovely still-life the broken teapot would make. She'd call it "Broken Dreams," and...

She realized the waiter had said something, and his smile held warmth, not annoyance. She smiled back for a second, then schooled her expression. Most of the people in the lounge had returned to their conversations or games, but a few looked at her, and they seemed irked. A familiar heavy and warmly itchy sensation swept through Veronica—shame.

"Silly V, silly V, says I'm a servant, look at me."

She mentally swatted the teasing childhood rhyme away and said, "I'm glad you're not hurt."

"I'm fine," he assured. "Now I should get the duchess a new set of tea and scones before she reports me to my supervisor." He bowed briefly to her and leaned toward her, so close as to almost be improper. "But I get off at six. Perhaps I can escort you around the deck?"

"No, sir, you may not." How dare he be so familiar? Well, she'd certainly invaded his space, but it had been an accident.

"Have a nice day then, Madame." He laughed and walked away. At least she hadn't hurt his pride too much.

When he left, Veronica turned around, slowly, not sure what to do. Head shakes and snickers followed her through the lounge, and she no longer found herself wanting to sit somewhere and have tea. Not with everyone watching and laughing at her. Well, not everyone...

"I just love my cabin," one woman gushed to another. "It's so spacious! I could have two other people over for tea, and it wouldn't seem cramped at all."

Veronica paused. She wanted to turn and ask where this spacious cabin was, but she didn't want to call further attention to herself after her double gaffe of causing an accident and being overly friendly with the staff.

Another woman responded to the first. "I heard they'd over-sold the first-class cabins, so they've been giving some people"—and the tone in which she said *some people* indicated that they would be less deserving—"some of the extra second-class compartments on this floor. The ones meant for servants."

"Right. We all know the good rooms are above."

"But what if there are second-class people here? Around us?"

"Oh, I'm sure they'll show their true colors, and then we can kick them downstairs."

"If they don't rally the wait staff to aid them." A group of titters followed that remark, and Veronica cringed, her cheeks burning. She dared not turn to see if they looked at her.

Well, that explained Veronica's cabin. She'd thought she was going first-class, though. Had Léonard messed up the reservation? Or was this one of his games to show her how she couldn't make it on her own without him?

The women's voices came closer, and Veronica ducked into an alcove, which happened to lead to the stairs down to the second-class—the acknowledged one, anyway. She descended halfway down so she could escape from having to face them, but then something else caught her attention—a woman's sobbing.

HENRY CAUGHT "MONSIEUR CLOUTIER'S" eye, whose exasperated facial expression likely mirrored his own. The maid—an American with brown skin and black hair—only sobbed when either of them tried to question her. Even the simplest query like, "What startled you?" produced a torrent of tears and a garbled answer that sounded like something about a "haint."

"Perhaps I can help," a young woman said. Henry looked up to see her descending the stairs and approaching the closet, where the maid crouched, wide-eyed. He thought she looked familiar. Ah, right, he'd noticed her when she boarded. Whoever she was, she had no business here. But then, did he? The captain had told him to look for secret pirates, not maids who thought they'd seen ghosts.

"I'm sorry," Henry told her, "but this is captain's business."

"And you're obviously not getting very far with it," she replied with a pleasant smile. Deceptively pleasant. Henry had seen that expression before, on the face of another woman who had argued with him, and if this young lady resembled that one in any way...

He'd heard an American expression of attracting more flies with honey than with vinegar, but he'd adjust it for her. The honey in her smile would hide poison if she were pushed.

"Please," Cloutier stood from his kneeling position beside

the maid and moved back. Davidson followed, reluctantly. The intruder knelt by the sobbing woman, her brown and copper-striped skirts pooling around her.

"Hello," she said and drew out the word. "My name is Veronica," she continued and gently took the woman's hands. "It sounds like you saw something that scared you."

Why didn't she just ask a direct question? Cloutier, possibly wondering the same, tensed, but Davidson put a hand on his arm. He knew enough about the Southern United States to recognize the tactic—start with the indirect query. He'd seen many a soldier disarmed by the charming strategy, and it seemed to work here as well. The maid's wails subsided to sniffles, and she looked up at Veronica with wet eyes.

"Th-there was a haint, Miss. A man with burning glass eyes." She shuddered and whispered, "He looked like the devil."

"So he was tall, then," Veronica said.

"Yes, and broad. And white-skinned."

"Pale like a haint who hasn't seen the sun," Veronica clarified.

"No, he'd seen the sun. Pale like him." She pointed to Cloutier. Henry arched an eyebrow, but she couldn't have mistaken the fake art dealer for a ghost. He'd been conversing with Henry at the time, after all.

"Did he look like him?" Veronica asked.

"N-no. He had a hat. And no scar."

Cloutier shifted, and Henry thought he heard a stifled sigh. Henry wondered if the other man hated being reduced to being the scarred man with the eyepatch. And understood. He'd often wondered if anyone would ever look at him as himself, not what he tried to get out of them or what he had lost.

Veronica squeezed the woman's hands. "Thank you for telling me. That's very helpful. Did he disappear?"

"No, he went down the hall. I think." She frowned. "I'm not sure. I covered my face, I was so scared."

Veronica glanced at Cloutier—did she know him?—and raised an eyebrow. He approached and held out his hands. Veronica and the maid each took one, and he helped them to their feet.

"You were very brave," Veronica assured the maid. "Do you mind telling me why these men upset you?"

The maid looked at her boots. "I'm sorry," she whispered. "I'm from a plantation. The master's sons..." Her shoulders shook, and Veronica put a hand on the shoulder closest to her.

"It must have been frightening to be in such a small space with them," she agreed, "especially after such a scare."

"Thank you for understanding, miss." She dropped a curtsey. "I have to get back to work." Then she darted away.

Henry wanted to ask a couple more questions, but he'd recognized the woman had reached the end of her limit. And she likely had work to do. Who knew what punishments she'd experienced in her previous life? He recognized the airship as a chance for reinvention for many of those aboard, including the maid. And possibly a chance for redemption for himself.

"That was well done." Cloutier's low voice thrummed in the air between them, and Henry stepped back, aware of how close they stood to this unmarried woman. No, she wore a wedding band. So where was her husband? Although he was no stranger to independent, free-spirited females, Henry still did not expect to encounter them randomly, and certainly not in a broom closet on an airship.

"Thank you." She looked up at Cloutier with lovely brown eyes, her cheeks pink. "I happen to know how to speak Southern."

Cloutier's cheek nearest Henry tensed as though it wanted to stretch his lips into a smile. Henry cleared his throat, and the two of them jumped apart.

"I believe we haven't been introduced," he said, eyeing both of them and challenging Cloutier. That would teach him for calling Henry rude. At least Henry hadn't neglected to introduce a woman.

"Monsieur Davidson, this is, ah..." Cloutier's face reddened, his scar standing out white against his ruddy cheek.

"Mrs. Veronica Kindred," she said and held out a hand.

"Charmed," Henry said. He carefully shook her hand, shocked by the coolness of the fabric of her glove. "Thank you for your help. Would you mind accompanying me to make a report to the captain?"

"I'd be delighted," she said, raising her chin.

Henry wondered several things in rapid succession. How old was she? She couldn't be more than mid-twenties. Again, where was her husband? She wore colors, not widow's weeds, although the colors of her dress were subdued enough to constitute partial mourning, so perhaps she'd been widowed for a while? And where did she get her confidence? Finally, would she end up being trouble for him?

Henry gestured for her to precede them through the hallway, and he caught an admiring expression on Cloutier's face when she turned. He followed Cloutier's gaze to her narrow waist and her small bustle, sensible for a ship's tight spaces. He didn't know what to think about the beautiful Mrs. Kindred, but he recognized one thing with certainty—she'd managed to capture Cloutier's attention. And, Henry would wager, the scarred man's heart would fall next. He'd seen such things happen before.

AFTER MADAME KINDRED had spoken to the maid, Luc finally identified the accent he'd heard in her French—American, but Southern. So she was a former Confederate, likely an expatriate who had escaped to Europe. That made her more than a glorified art thief. She had family connections. And money, most likely, although why would she be working? And what was she doing on the ship alone? He'd thought the older gentleman he'd seen her with at the airship dock had been her husband, but the man had handed her out of the carriage, supervised the unloading of the crates containing Luc's family heirlooms, and then driven off. There had been no sign of affection, but that didn't necessarily mean anything, especially in a couple of such disparate ages.

Now she preceded him through the narrow hallway and up the stairs, the inspector behind him. The implied rebuke at Luc failing to introduce the lovely woman to Henry stung. But then, Luc and she hadn't been formally introduced, either, although she'd allowed him to escort her on to the airship. Luc wanted to smack himself. Had he inadvertently slipped into the role of mysterious man in the eyepatch? He hated that role. In truth, he missed being the Marquis de Monceau, the man Paris bowed to, even if they thought he was his grandson. This new identity chafed.

He could beg off from the interview, but he loathed the idea of the lovely woman being alone with Davidson and the captain. Not that he had a reason to fear for her safety or virtue —he'd looked into Davidson when he'd been alerted as to the inspector's interest in him. Everything he'd managed to dig up on Davidson indicated the Englishman was a man of integrity, although too good at finding out things and not afraid to peek into the esoteric and mystical. Luc guessed the captain would be honorable as well. Luc admitted to himself that he envied Davidson's ease in his skin, especially since he knew from experience how women could fall for such confidence.

Luc didn't want Veronica Kindred to slip into any man's trap. Why? There was the question of his art, which he didn't want anyone else near. And another feeling stirred inside his chest cavity, which he'd thought had been emptied of any tender emotions since he'd been maimed. Blast. After he'd rescued her from the customs agent, he'd started feeling responsible for her. And that was not a sentiment he needed. It had gotten him in trouble before.

He stopped himself from rubbing his scar, and his face, which had started to stretch into an unfamiliar easy smile, snapped back into its customary scowl. Good. That's what he needed to do—be strong. Get what he needed and escape without attachments.

But what had the maid seen? Or who? Luc guessed that Le Rouge had a representative on board, sneaking around and spying on him. But it wasn't like that crew to be seen if they didn't want to be. Le Rouge appreciated stealth and cunning. Someone had been clumsy and likely would pay. Or perhaps a different pirate captain had an interest in the *Acadia Pearl*.

Davidson directed them to a hallway that led them not into the lounge, but to a different passageway between the lounge and dining room. Obviously not meant for passengers, the corridor was lined with wood of lower quality and had an unfinished look to it, although the sweet-chemical smell of varnish pervaded the space. Another staircase down brought them to the steering room and captain's office off to the side. Luc looked around, interested, at the many dials and the old-fashioned-looking ship's steering wheel, currently manned by a mate. He guessed the captain set the course and directed the airship upon takeoff and landing but then would supervise others in the task. Luc barely had time to take in all the dials, levers, and communication tubes before a cabin boy emerged from the captain's office, straightened his shirt, said with a cracked voice, "Captain Viero will see you now."

Luc took a quick look at the boy, noticing the flush in his cheeks. His very smooth cheeks under a forehead that had a feminine slant to it and big blue eyes with lashes slightly too long. The "boy" didn't look at him, just straight ahead, his pink lips pressed together. Luc wanted to ask him/her if he/she was all right, if the captain had hurt them. But he shook his head. Enough time for that later, and he was supposed to be keeping his own profile low. Still, he made a mental note to check on the young person later. Because that's what he did—rescue those who were helpless, even if he couldn't then save himself. He again resisted the urge to touch the scar on his cheek. Not that he could escape its reminder—he felt it every time the muscles under and around it moved, hence why he avoided smiling, which he couldn't do fully on that side. What was the point of smiling if others would only find him hideous?

The captain, a stout man with thick black hair and mustache, showed no sign of having just engaged in untoward extracurricular activities with the cabin boy. He looked up from his papers and gestured for them to come in. The dusky blue uniform of the French Airship League, a guild of air-farers, hugged his girth but had obviously been tailored to fit him. The brass buttons down the front shone in the light coming through the portholes behind the captain's desk and reflected in the mirrors to either side of the door. Luc had noticed several mirrors on the first-class floor, not so much on the lower ones, all, he presumed, to give the airship's inner spaces an illusion of more light.

"What's this, Davidson?" Captain Viero asked. "And who are these people?"

"This is Madame Veronica Kindred, one of your first-class passengers, and Stephan Cloutier, another one. We've just had a most unsettling experience."

Luc shook the captain's hand and pulled a chair back for Madame to sit. She seemed not to notice. She looked around, her expression one of curiosity. When he cleared his throat, she glanced up at him with her golden hazel eyes and gave him a small smile before taking the offered seat. He sat to one side of her, Davidson the other.

"Does this have anything to do with your task?" Viero asked

Davidson. That piqued Luc's interest—what business could the captain have with the inspector? And did it have anything to do with him or his former identity?

"I don't know." The inspector leaned back and crossed one leg over the other, ankle to knee, before he seemed to catch himself and sat straight. Interesting—he and the captain must be friends, or at least have some sort of familiarity with each other. And what task?

Luc was about to say something, but Madame spoke. "One of your staff saw something that disturbed them, Captain."

"Oh?" Viero's bushy black eyebrows rose, pushing wrinkles ahead of them up his forehead. Luc watched for signs of feigned surprise, but as far as he could tell, the expression seemed genuine. Or maybe it shocked him that Madame had spoken. Well, he'd continue to be surprised if that was the case. In the brief time Luc had known her, she'd proven to be a woman who knew her own mind and wasn't afraid to speak it.

"Yes, she said it looked like a—" She cleared her throat with an adorably ladylike sound and said, "'haint.' Some sort of ghost." She looked at Henry, who gestured for her to continue. "She said it was tall and pale, but not white. And looked like a man with shining eyes."

Henry and the captain exchanged glances.

"And when and where did this apparition occur?" Viero asked.

Henry answered, "About half an hour ago near the second-level broom closet close to the central stair."

"And did any of you see it?"

They all exchanged looks, although Luc knew they all had the same answer.

"No, sir," Luc said. "We all heard the scream and went to investigate."

Viero chuckled. "Just the three of you? Did no one else hear it? React?"

"Well, they may have," Madame said in a quivering voice, her cheeks flushed red, "but in my haste to discover the source of the scream, I may have, ah, distracted them by bumping into a waiter, causing him to drop the tray he was carrying. Perhaps the other passengers thought it had been me."

Viero laughed, his belly shaking. Luc exchanged a puzzled look with the others.

"Ah, I owe you a favor, Madame—what did you say your name is?"

"Veronica Kindred, Captain."

"If you did, indeed, manage to distract the other passengers, I appreciate it. You are aware that this is the inaugural voyage for our line, are you not?"

"Yes, Captain."

Luc arched an eyebrow at her seeming deference, then recognized her strategy. She'd dealt with overbearing men in her past and knew how to not ruffle feathers. Good.

"And everything needs to go smoothly to ensure the success of this endeavor." Viero steepled his fingers. "There will be some unhappy investors otherwise, including the new president of France." He again raised his eyebrows but focused his dark gaze on Davidson. "I trust our good Inspector Davidson will get things sorted out. Meanwhile, please enjoy your afternoon, and I would like for the three of you to join me for dinner. Also, Madame Kindred, please tell me, how is your room?"

"A little small, Captain." She leaned forward. "I can barely turn around in there."

"I believe I have a stateroom available on the top level. It's the show stateroom, but as I don't anticipate needing to display it, I'll have the steward move your things up there. Then we will be even, yes?"

"Thank you, Captain, that is very kind of you."

"Excellent. Well, then." He stood, and the three of them did likewise. "Ah, Monsieur Cloutier, I know I can depend on your discretion as well as yours, Madame."

They both nodded.

"Good. Expect the steward within the hour, Madame. I'll have the boy fetch one," the captain said. "If you have anything you'd like to move personally, please gather it up."

"Yes, Captain. And thank you."

They all made their farewells, and Davidson led them to the main deck, which circled the area with the lounge and dining room, two large spaces split by the central hallways.

"Thank you for escorting me, gentlemen," Madame said. "I need to gather my things."

"Are you sure you'll be all right?" Luc asked. "That was all...unsettling."

She looked up at him with a small grin. "I'm not afraid of ghosts, Monsieur."

5

———

Henry lingered behind when the others left and requested to speak to the captain. Viero looked up from his maps and charts when Henry walked in but didn't seem surprised.

Viero spoke before Henry could say anything. "Was it necessary to bring the two of them in?"

"I wanted you to get a look at Monsieur Cloutier." Henry remained standing, conscious of the fact he hadn't been invited to sit. Viero had a funny attitude about etiquette. Sometimes he seemed to care. Other times not. But Henry could never tell which mood he happened to be in at a given moment.

"What about him?"

"He looks like a pirate with that scar and eyepatch, but I can confirm he and I were speaking when the maid screamed, so he's not the 'haint,' as she called the apparition."

"And what happened to it after?"

"The girl said it disappeared, but she had also covered her eyes, so there's no telling where it—he—went."

"Interesting." Viero glanced over Henry's shoulder to one of the mirrors, and Henry wondered what view he sought. The last time Henry had checked, the variegated green squares of fields and vineyards spread out like a checkered carpet stained with the green of forests and the brown of hills. The coordinates had been calculated to bring them southward to catch the breezes that blew west. That was the only way the airship could make the journey without a prohibitive tonnage of coal. But if aether were to ever be turned into a power source rather than a weapon and method for summoning pagan gods, it would truly revolutionize the world.

"And what do you make of the girl?" Viero asked. "Sorry," he added when Henry raised his eyebrows. "Young woman?"

"She has her own secrets." Henry's sense of tragedy had tugged at him when she'd spoken. "But she was a tremendous help. As you could probably tell from her accent, she's from the former Confederacy. I'm guessing she's related to someone powerful, who sent her abroad to study until the war and its attendant dangers ended."

Viero nodded. "I looked at the passenger lists, specifically the cabin she described. It's an oddity on the lower first-class deck, originally meant for a maid accompanying a newlywed couple who wouldn't want a servant interrupting their newly wedded bliss." The sneer in Viero's voice told Henry what the captain thought of marriage. He gestured for Henry to come 'round the desk and join him. "She's booked under a Madame Basquet, not Kindred."

"Interesting. So she's connected to Léonard Basquet, infamous rogue art dealer and spy?"

"Yes. And he wanted to send us a message by using that name. Or perhaps he had designs on the girl—young woman— and she managed to evade him, so the cabin is a punishment."

"She's certainly attractive enough," Henry murmured.

"Ah, so you noticed?" Viero's wide grin lifted his mustache.

"I'm an alive male, of course I noticed," Henry snapped. "But she's not my preferred type. Granted, I do like a woman who can handle herself and is intelligent, but..." He shrugged in an imitation of what he'd seen the French do. "I prefer a woman with a more adventurous spirit." Dammit, he'd not been able to forget Davinia Crow since she'd dropped into his life and foiled his capture of rogue tinkerer Paul Farrell. Now there was a woman with a strong spirit.

"Ah, and did you see how Monsieur Cloutier looked at her?"

"Yes, perhaps I shouldn't have allowed him to escort her back to her cabin...." But he'd sensed that Cloutier wouldn't take advantage of her, at least not on the deck of an airship in broad daylight. And if his suspicions were true and Cloutier was the presumed deceased Marquis de Monceau, he knew the Marquis liked women, but he wouldn't do something to cause others to look at him too closely, other than the curiosity his injuries drew.

What had happened to the man? From what Henry had been able to glean about the Marquis and his interesting predecessors—no confirmed deaths on record, just a long line of gone aways and returns of sons—they had broad tastes but preferred to not be associated with too much scandal.

But that was a problem for a different day.

"But she can take care of herself," Viero said, bringing Henry's attention back to him. "I know her type. Capable. Has likely broken her share of hearts without realizing it."

"So she's a woman who doesn't want to be rescued," Henry guessed, wondering what Viero could know. It made sense—if he were to be the captain of an inaugural voyage of an airship, he would want to know everything he could about his passengers.

"Or who is waiting for the right one," Viero supplied. "And good luck to Cloutier."

"Right. Good luck to him."

THE AIR OUTSIDE had taken on the scent of the sea, and Veronica spotted a glimmer on the horizon. She swallowed against the anxiety that threatened to overtake her. On the other side of the ocean lay the newly re-United States of America. Her family. Her late husband's mother.

And all the expectations that Veronica would be the same girl that she'd been when she'd left. Everyone would be in for a surprise, but Veronica didn't know who would have the biggest challenge to overcome.

"What is it?" Cloutier asked. His biceps under her hand tensed.

"What is what?" she asked, looking up at him. She'd forgotten how tall he was, and he seemed to grow without the weight of ceilings overhead. The airship balloon blocked the sky, putting the deck in an almost perpetual shade depending on where one stood, but it didn't hold the same sense of heaviness. Or perhaps her mind played tricks on her.

"You stiffened as though you saw something." He looked around with a scowl. "What was it?"

"Nothing, just a thought. A memory." Of Peter lying on his deathbed, his confession... She shook her head. The years had passed, fading the recollection but not the sharp sting of betrayal, the knowledge of what he'd taken from her. And now, here, on this beautiful ship with all the interesting views and subjects, she didn't even want to try to capture any drawings. It would be too disheartening.

They rounded the corner that brought them to the back of the airship, and Veronica stopped. A young woman sat with her maid, both of them on crates. The maid embroidered something, but the young woman drew on a sketchpad. Her strokes, sure and dark, captured something. Although Veronica couldn't see what, she guessed. The ropes that tethered the gondola to the balloon? The vista below with fields that stretched to meet the sky? Veronica's fingers twitched, begging her to try. She sternly told them to stop. She knew their game. They'd only freeze when she held a pencil.

"Amateur," Cloutier snorted. "Everyone thinks they can draw, but so few can."

His condescending tone irked Veronica—how dare he dismiss the girl's efforts? "You're quick to pass judgment," she murmured, hoping the sound of the wind and the hum of the machinery underfoot kept the girl from hearing them. "You never know—she could be the next DaVinci, capturing the world with delicate lines and bringing to life things that men have only dreamed of with her blueprints and plans. Or catching moments to remember her trip by. Either way, she's obviously enjoying herself."

The airship turned, and the shadow line retreated, leaving them all in full sun. The maid stood and shaded her eyes.

"Mademoiselle, we should go inside. The sun will give you freckles."

The young woman looked up and squinted, then jumped to her feet when she saw Veronica and Cloutier.

"I am sorry," she said. "You startled me." Her gaze darted to Cloutier's face, and Veronica felt a tremor pass through him. She didn't think him so much a monster, and in spite of his attitude of a moment before, she now found herself with sympathy for him.

"What were you drawing?" he asked, surprising Veronica with his gentle curiosity.

"Oh, nothing, just the clouds and another ship." The girl showed them her drawing, and he practically snatched it away from her.

"Are you sure that's the shape of the balloon, that elongated oval?"

She nodded. "I am sure. I'd never seen one like it."

A shadow passed over the deck, and Veronica and the

others looked up, but the sun was too bright to allow them to look up for long.

"Please let me know if you see it again," he said and handed the pad back over. The girl gave him an odd look and scurried off, followed by her maid.

"What was it?" Veronica asked.

"Do you remember the airship that chased you at the chateau?"

She jerked away from him. "How did you know about that?"

He rubbed his temples. "You may think you were discreet, but you were being watched. You're not the only one who's interested in the contents of the Chateau Monceau."

Veronica stabbed a finger at him. "How dare you? Why didn't you tell me this earlier? What else do you know about me?" *How are you planning to hurt me?* She dropped her voice into a deadly low range. "Secrets can kill, Monsieur."

"I know, and I am sorry. I thought that, being associated with Léonard Basquet, you would know how cutthroat the Paris art world can be."

He had a point. Léonard had warned her that she might be followed, but that the burly men who accompanied her should keep her safe. As it turned out, only one of the men at the chateau had been useful, but she hadn't gotten a good look at her savior. Although he had seemed tall…

"You are right. I overreacted." With reason, but she wouldn't tell him that. "And since you know so much, do you know the identity of the man who saved me and my men from the airship?"

His mouth thinned, but he didn't say anything.

"You do know." She punched him on the arm. "Come on, tell me. I owe the man my life."

He put a finger on her lips. "Be careful what you say, Madame. Some men would be more inclined to use that against you than others."

Her lips tingled where his finger pressed against them, and her entire body heated at the casual intimacy of the gesture. She nodded, and he removed his hand from her face and stepped back, his expression unreadable. Did he recognize he'd been untowardly familiar? Or—the thought thrilled her—had he meant to be and had been looking for the right opportunity? She resisted the temptation to lick her lips to see what his skin would taste like. It had been so long, and...

And that way would lead to betrayal and heartbreak. She straightened her hat and turned. "Good afternoon, Monsieur. I need to meet the steward in my cabin. There is a certain picture I don't want him to disturb." Especially since the thing seemed to have a mind of its own. Not that she believed in such super- stitious nonsense—the motion of the airship was likely to blame for its antics earlier. At least that's what she kept telling herself.

"What painting would that be?" Cloutier asked.

Veronica cocked her head at him. Why was he so curious? "I am not going to invite you back to my cabin, Monsieur. I will show it to you another time."

He closed the distance between them. "But please, do me this favor. Whatever happens, don't show it to anyone else. Just me."

The intense expression in his one remaining eye tugged a nod from her. "I promise."

He stood just inches from her, and she resisted the urge to see what his lips would taste like. She wasn't that kind of woman, and she wouldn't fall into the trap of becoming a merry widow known for her indiscretions, not her expertise. Not when she had so much else to accomplish.

With a sharp nod, he stepped back, then turned on his heel and walked away. She shook her head. There was something about him... For the first time, she found herself wondering what sort of secrets Monsieur Stephan Cloutier kept.

S*TUPID*, *stupid, stupid...*

Luc's steps set a drumbeat for his thoughts. What had he been thinking, touching her like that? Yes, she'd had her hand on his arm, but that was within the bounds of propriety. Touching her lips was not. Especially since that one contact had made the rest of him envy the tip of his finger. The sun had blazed in her eyes, making them more golden, and she'd seemed ethereal, which had made her irresistible. He'd long ago come to recognize the desire for a woman who matched him in a unique and fundamental way—different from the rest of the human race, but hidden among them, a ruby among the rocks. But she couldn't be that gem for him. His life was not his own, as the appearance of La Belle Rouge had reminded him. If the captain had wanted to stay hidden, he would have. The appearance of the ship in the girl's picture—and the shadow in front of the sun, likely that very ship—had served its purpose. Luc knew he was being followed.

As for the ghost in the hold... Luc would conduct his own investigations. Not that he could do much subtly. The young artist's reaction had reminded him how hideous he appeared to others. It was a wonder Veronica didn't shy away from him. And now that he thought about it, she hadn't, even at their first meeting. She had measured him up with understandable curiosity but had not reacted outwardly to his eyepatch or scar. And she hadn't recognized him at the chateau. Good. She wouldn't suspect he needed to steal his art back.

Once he turned the corner, he found an alcove to hide in. He hated to follow her like a sneak, but he needed to see what piece she'd deemed too valuable to trust to the stewards. Could that be his missing clue? She'd already demonstrated that she saw things differently from others—himself included. And Léonard Basquet had trusted her to choose what she brought back from the chateau. Basquet might be a dirty old man, but Luc knew he wasn't a fool. No matter what Basquet wanted from her, he wouldn't send an amateur on an important errand.

A pattering of light footsteps made him shrink further into the shadows, feeling even more like a monster having to hide. Veronica came around the corner, accompanied by the girl with the sketch pad and the maid. Luc noticed the strain at the corner of Veronica's eyes and mouth. It pained her to talk to the girl, who seemed not to notice and showed off her drawings as they walked. Interesting. Were the girl's attempts that bad? Luc hadn't noticed anything overtly awful. The girl had talent but was untrained, or had been trained badly, but with practice would get better. And Veronica had defended her. So what bothered her so much about the conversation?

Not that it was any of his business, but, curiosity piqued, he slipped from his hiding spot and followed them, careful to place his feet so as to minimize any sounds. The young artist and the maid went back into the lounge, and Veronica continued to the door that led to the lower level of first-class cabins. The lights in that part of the corridor had either burned out or been turned off, cloaking the space in thick dimness. She looked up, sighed, and pressed on. Luc followed her but stopped. A shadow detached itself from the wall after she'd passed by the housekeeping closet. Had it been hiding inside the closet?

Luc made his progress even quieter. What did this person want? Was it the "haint" the maid had seen below? Or a different threat?

He wanted to warn Veronica, but he didn't want to startle her pursuer into doing something desperate because he'd be cornered by the two of them. Instead, Luc followed them until Veronica went into her cabin and shut the door, perhaps more firmly than was necessary. Good, she'd sensed something amiss. Hopefully she wouldn't come out too soon.

The shadow paused outside her door, and in a stray beam of diluted sunlight from one of the windows at the end of the corridor, the shape of a tall man came into view. He wore goggles with a red light emanating from them. The "haint," indeed, and it was after her. How long before it would pretend to be the steward and she'd open her door to it? That would never do. Luc pulled a knife from one boot.

"What do you want, Monsieur?" Luc asked, stepping closer. He twisted his wrist, allowing light to glint off the blade.

The man turned and asked in a strange voice, "Who are you?"

"The more pertinent question is who you are and what you want with the young lady?" Luc attempted to maintain a relaxed posture while preparing for a fight.

He didn't have much room to maneuver and didn't know if the man was armed. A sliver of light behind the intruder indicated that Veronica had opened her door.

The man took advantage of Luc's distraction to lunge, but he grunted and stumbled forward, and something metal clanged to the ground.

"'Ey, what're you doing there?" A gruff voice yelled from behind Luc. The intruder stumbled to his feet, then lurched away down the hall. Luc started after him but stepped in the—thankfully unused—chamber pot that Veronica had hit the man with. Two burly stewards grabbed him by the arms.

"I'm not the man you're after, you fools," Luc said. "He ran down the corridor."

"Sure he did," the one who'd yelled at him said. "You weren't bothering this young lady 'ere at all."

"No, it was a different man," Veronica said. "I saw him. If you examine this one, you'll see he doesn't have a bump on his head from where I hit him with the, ah..." She gestured to the chamber pot, still stuck to Luc's foot.

One of the stewards took off down the corridor while the

other one confirmed that Luc indeed lacked a bump on his head.

"Sorry, sir," the steward said. "Now, Madame, may we help you move your things?"

Luc didn't know if he was included in the "we," but he decided to stick around and be helpful. Just in case the intruder returned, of course. His altruism had nothing to do with the painting in Veronica's room, the one she didn't trust the stewards to move. Or the fact she'd almost just been attacked and he wanted to make sure she was all right.

She carried the painting into the hallway, and he restrained himself from holding out his hands in a request to take a closer look. She held the picture of his great-grandfather as a boy with a golden ball. It had no artist's signature, and Luc had never thought it to be that valuable, but...

"So that's the one you wanted to handle yourself?" he asked, attempting to sound casual.

"Yes," she said and looked down at it with a wistful smile. "There's something about this little boy. It's not at all a masterful piece, probably not of any value beyond its age, but it's winsome, isn't it?"

Luc didn't recall his great grandfather as anything resembling "winsome," but by the time Luc had met him, the young boy had grown into a fearsome old man who raved about the family legacy and cautioned Luc every time he saw him to never tell anyone about his true age. Luc didn't know how old his ancestor had been when he'd died, only that the villagers of Luc's childhood never saw him. Family visits were always kept secret in case someone saw and got suspicious. Not that many people would know. At the time his great grandfather had built the Chateau Monceau, it had been far away from the village of Monceau, and farther yet from Paris.

"I suppose you could say so," Luc agreed, if only to keep her talking. What did she notice about it? He'd looked at the child and the ball so many times he could bring the image to mind with the clarity one typically reserved for very special memories. "Did you discover ıanything unusual about the painting? Besides its age?"

The steward grunted under the weight of Veronica's trunk, and Luc helped him to bring it up to the stateroom, which was, as promised, the height of luxury. A maid who had been putting sheets on the bed curtsied and scrambled out of the way when she saw them, but Veronica put a hand on her arm to stop her.

"Are you all right now?" she asked. Luc realized it was the maid from earlier.

"Yes, miss."

"Did the thing you saw have glowing red eyes?" Luc asked. He thought he remembered her saying something like that but couldn't recall exactly.

The maid darted a glance to the steward, who watched the exchange with a curious expression.

"I can't say I saw anything," the maid said with a lift of her chin, and she walked out.

Veronica huffed at Luc, and he recognized his blunder. He'd failed to be considerate of how the maid would be looked at or treated by her fellow staff members.

Luc and the steward put the chest in the corner, and Veronica placed the painting against the wall on the nightstand by the bed. A sunbeam hit it, and Luc noticed that the ball wasn't a solid golden color. He picked up the painting and examined it. The shadows on the ball seemed too regular in shape to be mere marks to indicate light. Indentations perhaps?

"Do you see them, too?" Veronica asked.

"The designs on the ball? Yes."

"What do you make of them, Monsieur Cloutier?"

Luc didn't want to say. A small bud of hope had bloomed in the center of his chest. Could this be the clue he sought?

"I wanted to find something to clean the surface," Veronica said. "As you can see, it hasn't been well cared-for."

"You mustn't." Luc clutched the painting. "The substances used to clean a ship are too harsh for a delicate job like this."

"You didn't let me finish," she chided. "I recognized that once I saw the contents of the cleaning closet when I was comforting the maid. Besides, the marks seem to come clearer every time the sun touches the painting." She gently took it from him and brought it back to the sunbeam. "It's like the sunlight brings out the detail, but in more ways than one would expect. I don't want to leave it in the direct light too long, though. It may fade."

Luc wanted to snatch the picture from her but dared not. It would only arouse her suspicions.

"Come," he said. "We should report to the captain about the man who..." He was about to say, "Followed and surprised you," but then he'd have to admit he'd been following her.

"Was lurking in the hallway?" She looked up at him with an arched eyebrow. "Thank you for keeping him from, well, whatever he was going to do."

"You're welcome. And that was quick thinking with the chamber pot, although you should have stayed in your cabin."

"I haven't gotten as far as I have by hiding away from my problems, Monsieur." She crossed her arms. "Well, not always. But yes, we should report to the captain."

He preceded her out of the room and watched her lock the door. She slipped the key on its chain over her head. He wondered what he would need to do to get the painting away from her. And then figure out what to do with it.

6

———

Veronica followed Monsieur Cloutier out of the passenger corridor. Now that she'd been in the true luxury suites, she could appreciate how cramped the lower floor had been. She'd barely had enough light to see her room number, after all. Why had Léonard booked such a small room for her? Had he known? Was he punishing her for refusing his proposal? She shuddered at the thought of being married to him, another man who would try to steer her activities in a direction he deemed "appropriate" rather than allowing her—ugh, she hated that word, "allowing"—to follow her own desires.

Or had he been protecting her, hiding her in a small room that was difficult to find? Someone had found it, obviously. As had Monsieur Cloutier. What did he want? And how, truly, had he known about the attack on the chateau? She could believe the men who worked for Léonard had blabbed in the bars and taverns that night in spite of his swearing them to silence. One didn't barely get away with one's life and not talk about it, especially in such a dramatic situation.

She shivered when she remembered the feeling of being

followed. A cloud of panic had covered her like the shadow of the airship at the chateau. She'd heard Cloutier confront the man, and that's when she'd stumbled over the chamber pot. It had had a note in it that sometimes the airship plumbing failed, so each room had a chamber pot as backup. Lacking any other weapon, she'd used what she had.

What had Léonard gotten her into? Veronica's head spun with the different possibilities, the different scenarios. She'd never felt such confusion when she'd been drawing. The pictures had seemed to flow from her fingers without her brain getting in the way. Now her brain refused to relinquish control. Could that be the source of her blocked abilities—her brain wanting her to stay in control at all times so something bad wouldn't happen?

Henry Davidson was just emerging from the captain's office when they arrived, and he raised his eyebrows, but that was the only measure of surprise he displayed. Veronica admired his restraint—no trouble with control there. She imagined the inside of his head looking like a clockwork mechanism, the emotions ticking through in their proper manners and times.

"Is everything all right?" Davidson asked, although he must know it wasn't. Veronica hid a smile at his English politeness.

"Madame Kindred has been attacked," Cloutier said.

Davidson looked Veronica over, but not in the way men often took in her slim figure and symmetrical, if not beautiful, face. Or that was how she saw herself, anyway.

"I am not injured, Inspector, thanks to the quick thinking of Monsieur Cloutier, who happened to be in the corridor at the time." She hoped Davidson didn't think they'd snuck away for a tryst.

"And Madame Kindred's ability to wield unusual weapons," Cloutier said, the twist of his lips approaching a grin.

Davidson ushered them into the captain's office. Viero did not look happy to see them, his bushy black brows sinking toward the bridge of his nose. Veronica again felt the presence of *something* valuable beneath where they stood. Yet another mystery.

"I heard what you said out there," Viero told them. "Please, have a seat and give me the details."

"I had just walked into the corridor to my previous room intending to gather my things," Veronica said, "when I felt like someone watched me."

"Did you hear anything?" Davidson asked.

Veronica frowned, bringing herself back to the gloom and the sense of wrongness. "Yes, a click, but not footsteps."

"And then what?"

"I moved quickly to my room—whatever was watching me seemed to be between me and the door to the deck—and locked myself in. Before I closed the door, I looked behind me and saw a pair of glowing red eyes. It put me in mind of the 'haint' the maid said she saw."

"And Monsieur Cloutier, why don't you catch us up on what you saw to that point?" Davidson asked. He took notes on a little pad of paper he'd produced from his pocket. With a spark of amusement, Veronica thought it interesting how he'd snapped straight into detective mode.

What did she revert to when the situation called for? An artist? Yes, one who couldn't produce art.

Cloutier cleared his throat. "I allowed Madame Kindred time to return to her room so as to not give any sense of impropriety, and when I entered the hallway, I saw a man step out of the cleaning closet and follow her. I didn't know if he was armed, so I didn't want to startle him." He related how he'd confronted the intruder in front of Veronica's room and then how she'd used the chamber pot in her room to temporarily incapacitate him. He confirmed that what Veronica and the maid had seen were glowing red goggles.

Davidson nodded. "I know of an inventor in the States who

developed something similar for seeing better in the dark. Something about the wavelength of the light making it easier for the eye to perceive objects in dimness. I wasn't aware they'd become widely available."

Viero, who'd listened with his chin propped on steepled fingers, chimed in, "Our military has been working on goggles like those for use underwater. We can argue the origin of the device all day, but the question is, why did this person follow you, Madame Kindred?"

Veronica's brain had been skipping around the question. "I don't know," she said. "Truly, I don't. But this isn't the first time I've been targeted."

"What do you mean?" Davidson's pencil, which hadn't stopped moving, stood poised above the pad.

Veronica told them about the pirate ship attack at the Chateau Monceau, and the writing utensil danced across the paper once again. She didn't leave out the part where she'd grabbed the reins. Why should she? She'd saved them, although she suspected the men who'd been with her had changed that part of the story in the retelling. She addressed the captain and Davidson, but in her peripheral vision she caught sight of Cloutier nodding occasionally as though what she said checked out with his recollection, not the version she thought had been relayed. But how would he know? He'd denied being there.

Or perhaps he was lying. Had he now helped her twice?

When she finished, Davidson looked at Viero, who muttered, "Blasted pirates."

"You need to tell them, at least her," Davidson urged.

With a heavy sigh, Viero said, "We'd received notice of pirates targeting passenger airships over the Atlantic. The method of the attack showed they had some connection inside the ship. But not an intruder, someone on the crew." He shook his head. "I wonder if we should land, but there is too much riding on this journey."

"I feel more secure in my new quarters," Veronica put in. "It seems that if you were to land and make everyone disembark that the intruder could slip out with everyone else."

"She has a point," Davidson said. "I will continue to investigate."

"Subtly," Viero urged. "I cannot allow the passengers to know about this, especially not the first-class passengers. Consequently, I can't station someone in front of your room, Madame, but I can increase the frequency of the security officers' patrols. They're too fond of looking out of their window and drinking wine, anyway."

"Are the passengers in danger?" Cloutier asked.

"Not that we can tell," Davidson admitted. "While this person has appeared, he hasn't attacked anyone without provocation." He held up a hand when Cloutier leaned forward, his mouth open. "You confronted him. Yes, his actions look suspicious. But we don't know what he wants, and Madame is right. We're not going to find out unless we can catch him in the act and capture him."

"Monsieur Cloutier, would you excuse us?" the captain asked. Cloutier nodded and left.

"Madame," Viero said, and Veronica turned her attention back to him. She hadn't realized, but she'd watched Cloutier leave.

"Yes, captain?"

"Are you certain that the man who followed you in a threatening manner was not Monsieur Cloutier?"

"Yes." Veronica nodded to emphasize her answer. "I heard the two of them talking, and I saw Cloutier jump back when I bashed the other one on the head."

"And what did you say you hit him with?" Davidson asked.

Veronica hoped she didn't blush, but the warmth that came

to her face told her otherwise. "My chamber pot. By the way, I appreciate the washroom chamber in the new quarters."

Davidson laughed, his face made gentle by his amusement. The captain coughed.

"Good," Davidson said, "Well, yes, I just needed to make sure it wasn't Cloutier."

Veronica nodded. "Oh, don't get me wrong, captain. Cloutier has his secrets, but I don't think I figure in any of them." But as she said the words, something rang false about them.

HENRY ESCORTED Madame Kindred out of the crew area and back to her room.

"After all the excitement I need to lie down," she said. He found the order of her words interesting, like she'd spent a lot of time among the French, although she obviously came from the former Confederate states. He wondered what about her had attracted the infamous Léonard Basquet, known for his disdain of Americans in general and Southerners in particular. And what she had done to make him stick her in the maid's quarters.

"Do you have a maid or someone I can send to help you?" Henry asked.

She looked down and shook her head. "I'm all alone on this journey, Monsieur Davidson."

And again, her words hinted at something else, another meaning. He took his leave of her but pondered the exchange all afternoon, frustrated that being on an airship kept him from reaching out to contacts and further looking into Madame Kindred. The more he interacted with her, the more of a conundrum she became. The same for Monsieur Cloutier, whom Henry spotted in the lounge.

The scarred man sat alone in a chair grouping of four, a brandy at his elbow and a paper in his hands. He was scowling at something, or did his face always look like that at rest? Henry had observed that when some people were thinking or concentrating hard on something—or even daydreaming—their face hardened into an angry expression. That's why he'd schooled his own facial muscles to be carefully neutral when he was not reacting to something, and even then, he tried to choose his expressions carefully. He'd once felt comfortable with someone, but... No, he wouldn't track backward into memory. The way now went forward, and he had two interesting mysteries—the intruder on the ship and Madame Kindred.

As for Cloutier... Henry couldn't stop himself from approaching the man.

Cloutier looked up when Henry's shadow fell across his paper, and Henry had no doubt the art dealer meant his current scowl for Henry.

"Is Madame all right?" Cloutier asked.

"Yes, she's in her room. Resting."

"Good." Cloutier shook the paper and closed it before Henry could get a peek at what had engrossed him. Cloutier picked up his brandy and took a sip.

"How are you after the attack?" Henry asked.

Cloutier shrugged. "As well as could be expected. At least I wasn't the one bashed by a chamber pot."

"Clever woman, that." Henry sat without being invited. He didn't want Cloutier to feel uncomfortable with Henry standing over him. He sensed his being there disconcerted Cloutier. It remained to be seen whether being thrown off would cause Cloutier to talk or clam up.

"Perhaps too clever," Cloutier agreed. "I had the situation under control." The slide of his gaze told Henry he lied. Interesting.

"And what were you doing in the lower first-class corridor? I saw your ticket is for the upper deck. It has its own entrance stairs."

Cloutier shrugged. "Exploring. If I'm going to be stuck on this airship for a week, I want to know about it."

A flimsy reason, but Henry didn't press. He suspected Cloutier had been following Madame Kindred, but why? He'd obviously not meant to harm her. Or had he?

"What are you drinking?" Henry asked, hoping he could get the man to take another sip, loosen his tongue further.

"Brandy." He named a somewhat obscure house that Henry knew to be the Marquis de Monceau's favorite.

"I've not tried it," Henry lied. "How is it?"

Good, another sip. "Smooth." He put the glass on the side table. "If you don't mind, Mister Davidson, I was rather enjoying my paper. It's helping me to settle after the events of earlier."

Henry rose, the hint taken. He'd see what else the man had to say at dinner that night when wine might blur his caution.

Henry spent the rest of the afternoon prowling around the airship. The small second-class deck was crowded but clean, and unlike on a regular ship, had plenty of light and air, although the exterior decks were too small for any sort of furniture. He poked around the cargo part of the hold and didn't find anything suspicious or interesting. Indeed, his search turned up nothing—no place where someone could hide away, although he suspected that might change after a couple of nights. The intruder would have to sleep somewhere if he'd stowed away. Or—and this would make finding him more difficult—perhaps he was a passenger or a crew member. Henry had observed the ship's security upon boarding and had seen how tight it was, so that would make more sense. And customs agents had examined all of the cargo.

But they could be bribed.

Dinnertime approached, and Henry returned to his cabin

to freshen up. He would arrive early and report his findings—or lack thereof—to Viero. Then he could see how Madame Kindred and Monsieur Cloutier behaved.

When Henry walked into the dining room, which had been made even more formal for dinner, he spotted Viero talking to a couple Henry recognized from the first-class lounge.

"Brilliant start to the journey, Captain," the man trumpeted through a ridiculously large mustache. "Brilliant start. I have to say, this is so much more comfortable than going by steamship."

"And no airsickness?" Viero asked.

The woman shook her tower of blonde curls. "Not at all, captain. As my husband said, so much more comfortable. I simply could not abide all the motion of a boat or train."

"This is the best way to travel," her husband agreed. "Although I'll reserve my judgment until I can test the quality of your dinner service." He patted his belly, which looked like it didn't discriminate too much about what went in it.

Henry hovered in the shadows behind the trio, and Viero caught his eye.

"I'm sure you'll not find it to be lacking," Viero told them. "Ah, I see our maître'd has an excellent table waiting for you. Enjoy your dinner, Your Graces."

Ah, a duke and duchess. Henry had recognized the accent as English, but due to his work taking him out of the country for most of the year, he knew most of the nobility by name, not by face. Good to know about the potential targets of untoward actions.

Viero gestured for Henry to join him at the captain's table, which was simply an unassuming table in the corner between two walls, no windows. "We wanted to save the best tables for the passengers," Viero said. "And I can't stand feeling like I'm in a fishbowl, especially when I can't see out of the windows at night."

"Understandable," Henry agreed. He, too, felt protected by the walls. Interesting. He thought he'd like all the windows, but he felt exposed even though he knew there was nothing beyond them but clouds and sky. At least that's what he hoped.

Viero shook his head when Henry told him of his suspicions that the intruder who'd surprised the maid was a passenger or crew member.

"Impossible," Viero huffed. "I told you how important it was that this voyage went well. We got dossiers on everyone except that Monsieur Cloutier, who was a last-minute addition, and who cannot be the intruder since he was there on both occasions."

"Even all of the second-class passengers?" Henry asked.

"Yes, even them. The Republic has eyes everywhere."

Henry didn't comment on the moral difficulty of a government spying on its people. No one in France trusted anyone else after the last round of troubles. And if Cloutier had gotten on without being vetted first, then he suspected others might have as well.

A ripple of murmurs made him direct his attention to the door of the dining room, where Veronica Kindred had just entered. She wore a gown of deep green in the French style, which left her arms below her elbows and her chest bare, although the scooped collar's black lace hid the dent of her cleavage, and she wore black satin gloves. She had a hairpiece with peacock feathers and jewels that sparkled like emeralds tucked into her light brown upswept curls. Henry guessed the "jewels" were probably paste, but they made for a striking effect. It was still the cocktail hour, and people stood around in clumps by their tables. As Veronica passed, the other passengers turned their backs to her and otherwise deliberately ignored her.

"Apparently you didn't screen for politeness," Henry murmured.

Viero frowned, the lines beside his mouth deepening. "What could the poor girl have done to deserve that?"

"You're assuming she did anything. But she did bump the waiter earlier. Perhaps she delayed someone's tea."

"True. People can be needlessly cruel." Still, Viero didn't move to approach her or wave her over, although Henry guessed that some small gesture of approval from the captain would go a long way with the disgruntled passengers. When Madame Kindred saw him, she started to smile, then, hesitated.

"Madame, over here," Henry said and walked to her. "May I escort you to the captain's table?" he asked, pointedly and possibly too loudly.

"Yes, thank you."

Viero had thankfully recovered himself and greeted her warmly.

"You look lovely this evening, Madame," Viero said. Davidson noticed how the captain could turn his charm on and off. Right now he oozed it, not at all giving the impression that he'd been reluctant to welcome Madame Kindred to their table.

"Thank you," she murmured, and she shot Henry a wink. He reminded himself that although she looked young and untested, he needed to not underestimate her. She likely caught on to more than any of them realized.

Henry held a chair out for Madame and heard the captain welcoming Monsieur Cloutier. The man cut a dashing figure in his evening dress, and Henry again got the strong sense of déjà vu. If Cloutierwasn't at least related to the Marquis, if not the Marquis himself, Henry would eat his gloves. But how could anyone have survived the airship crash that had lit up Paris on that dark winter night and littered its streets with carnage?

The assembled diners took their seats, and Viero stood in front of the table to say a few words. Henry paid scant attention. He couldn't help but notice that Cloutier and Madame ignored each other, had barely greeted each other. Now she looked up at the captain, her gaze fixed at the back of his head, and Cloutier studied his menu, which laid out the four courses and wines on a rectangular piece of vellum.

Henry joined in the polite applause, and Viero took his seat. None of them sat with their back toward the room, so Henry knew they could all feel, if not see, the disapproving glances sent their way. He had to give Viero credit for not giving into social pressure and disinviting Cloutier and Madame from the table, but he wondered what social damage had been incurred. And if the voyage would feel much longer than the week it should take.

The waiters brought the first course, a French onion soup. The rich, savory smell made Henry's stomach growl, and he looked around to see if anyone noticed. Madame put a hand to her own middle and Cloutier's mouth twitched.

"Perhaps you should ask the head of hospitality to make teatime heavier, Captain," Cloutier commented.

"It's just that everything smells so wonderful," Madame said. "You're truly going beyond what anyone hoped for with this ship."

"Thank you." Viero raised his wine glass. "To old friends and new. May the magic in our journey be a joy to us all."

Henry clinked his glasses with the others. "So tell us, Madame," he said. "What brings you aboard the *Acadia Pearl*?"

"I'm escorting a small art collection to the new museum in Terminus." Her face lit with a grin. "I'm to be the co-director."

"I didn't know you were an art expert," Viero lied. Of course he knew. He had dossiers on all the passengers.

"I studied in London and then in Paris," she replied. Henry noticed she didn't mention Léonard Basquet.

"And where did the art come from?" Cloutier asked. "A private collection?"

She looked at him with surprise, as though he should know. "Yes, from a requisitioned property. The Chateau Monceau."

"Ah, bad business, that," Viero commented. "Poor man. Sounds like his skirt-chasing got the better of him in the end."

"How so?" Madame asked just as Cloutier said, "That's just a rumor."

"He was running away with a widow, or so the story goes." Viero shook his head. "They were attempting to escape from the Prussians, but they couldn't escape death."

Henry watched Cloutier's face during the exchange. His expression was more shuttered than usual, and his jaw muscles tightened.

"Had you ever met him?" Madame asked.

Viero chuckled. "No, but I'd heard about him. That Madame Cinsault had quite the reputation. It wasn't surprising she managed to trap him. Or perhaps they ensnared each other. Either way, they got what was coming to them. She wasn't well-liked among the air industry. We all knew she directed Cinsault Shipping through her husband. Poor man. He'd been murdered just before she died."

"Murdered!" Madame leaned forward and put down her spoon. "This sounds like a penny dreadful, Captain."

Cloutier cleared his throat. "If penny dreadfuls were made up of rumors and hearsay. Can we not show some respect for the dead?"

Viero looked like he wanted to argue, but he picked up his wine glass and swirled. "As you wish, Monsieur. And what brings you on this journey? You're an art dealer, as I recall."

Cloutier looked beyond Henry to a window, but a quick glance behind him only showed Henry their reflections.

"Yes, I'm after a certain treasure, but I can't say more," Cloutier said. For the barest moment, a wistful expression flitted across his face before he resumed his normal scowl. "But at this point, I'm not sure what I would do even if I were to find it."

7

Veronica pondered Cloutier's words through the evening and into the next morning. Somehow she wasn't surprised when she went into the breakfast room and found him waiting, two settings at his table. He acknowledged her with a nod but didn't wave her over. She looked around for somewhere else to sit, anywhere else, but the cold stares and turned shoulders told her the other patrons didn't welcome her. When he saw her approach, he stood and pulled out the chair for her. With a sigh, she joined him at his table.

"We're over open water now," he said with a shudder, although the corner of his mouth on the non-scarred side of his face quirked upward. "No going back now."

"Or soon going back will be harder than going forward." She nodded to the waiter who hovered with a silver coffee urn. She took a deep breath as the rich black liquid poured into her cup, savoring the earthy smell. She hoped it would clear the fog and the lingering odor of herbal incense smoke that had haunted her dreams. She wondered if the light pouring through the windows highlighted the nightmare-stamped dark circles under her eyes. Perhaps her haggard appearance was responsible for the other passengers' rejection of her. But she knew that wasn't the case.

Her daytime fear had come true—she'd been marked a merry widow, and the female passengers would shun her in order to keep her away from their husbands. Meanwhile, she would have to fend off the unwanted advances of the male passengers. Joining one of the few single men aboard for breakfast wouldn't help, but the damage had likely been done the day before.

"How did you sleep?" Cloutier asked after she'd put in her order for a soft-boiled egg and toast. He ordered bangers and mash.

"Wretchedly," she said, too tired to pretend. "You?"

"Decently."

Blast him, he seemed amused. At least he didn't seem too interested in further conversation. She ate her breakfast in silence, and although he'd apparently finished eating before she arrived, he stayed. She wished he would go—his presence didn't help her reputation. Or her nerves when she recalled her body's reaction at his teasing touch the day before.

Once she finished, he stood and held out a hand. "May I escort you on a turn around the deck?"

She glanced around. The women continued to appear to ignore her, but she could almost feel their attention and curiosity. Did some of the men look at her with leers?

Perhaps allying herself with Cloutier would be a smart move? Or would it worsen her reputation?

An electric tingle at the back of her neck told her that someone watched her. She turned to see the girl who'd been drawing on the deck. The little minx winked at her, and Veronica knew who had been spreading rumors about her and Cloutier. The fact that they'd shared a semi-intimate moment didn't help. Blast it all, she'd messed up again.

With a sigh, she nodded and accepted his offer.

LUC ESCORTED Madame out of the ship's dining room. He noticed the disapproving sniffs, but at least the two men who had been making eyes at her turned away when he passed, their jaws set. He'd wanted to give her space, to allow her to come to him in her own time, but he couldn't leave her to the wolves. He'd known their types. Had been their type, although he'd never married. They'd get away from their wives and attempt to corner her, then deny anything if she were to make a complaint against them later. Their long-suffering wives would provide an alibi.

He hated other men sometimes.

"I didn't want to cause scandal, Monsieur," she said once they were out in the open air. Her sigh moved her breast against his arm, and he tried not to react to the stab of desire the small contact sent through him.

"You being on the ship alone is scandal enough, Madame." Indeed, he could almost be angry at her presumably dead husband. "Did you not have a companion you could convince to travel with you?"

She snorted. "You know very little of me, Monsieur."

He couldn't argue. Nor could he deny that he wanted to know more with each passing hour they spent together. What a fool he acted, thought...felt. He'd had many women in his time, and his past conquests would have to be enough. His missing eye and scar marked him as damaged and dangerous. What respectable woman would look at him twice? And since when did he care about what respectable women thought of him? Not all of them, just this one. Because she had something else he wanted. At least that's what he told himself.

He glanced down to see she'd turned her light brown eyes

up toward his face, and she didn't flinch away. The words he'd been about to say dried up in the almost gold of her eyes.

"And I don't know much of you," she said with a shrug. "We both have our secrets, Monsieur."

They turned the corner to the spot where the young woman had been drawing the day before. Had it only been a day? It felt like much longer. Madame drew away from him and looked out from near where the girl had sat. "I can see why she positioned herself here. The view is lovely on all sides."

"Do you draw, Madame?" He noticed the fingers of her right hand twitching.

She clasped her hands together and kept her gaze fixed on the ocean below the deck. "No. That is, not anymore."

"I'm sorry to have upset you."

She wiped her eyes. "No, it's not your fault. My husband..." She shook her head.

"Right." Her husband had probably been a perfect young man, supportive of his wife's dreams and talent. Meanwhile, Luc, the cad, had to talk himself out of attempting to seduce her. "I'm sorry. Did he die recently?" And how had she gotten mixed up with Léonard Basquet?

"No." She brushed a stray honey-colored curl out of her face. "It was a few years ago. In Terminus. Before I came to work with Léonard Basquet in London. Do you know him?"

Luc shrugged. "I've heard the name. Your husband knew him?"

"Yes, he'd studied under him. But hadn't had any talent for finding good art, so he returned to Terminus and started a school. And then the war began. And wouldn't end."

Luc did the mental math. "Your husband must have been much older than you."

"A decade and a half." She came to join him. "But he was determined, and so was I."

He could definitely describe her as determined. And she seemed to like older men. If only she knew...

She yawned. "I'm sorry. It's not you. I need to lie down for a bit."

"I'll escort you back to your room."

"No, that's all right." Then she paused. He guessed that she, too, remembered the man in the corridor. "Well, if you wouldn't mind."

"I'll go with you as far as the top of the stairs."

"Thank you."

ONCE LUC MADE sure Madame had made it to her room safely, he walked around the deck a couple more times. The angle of the morning sun turned half the promenade into an oven. Most of the passengers escaped inside the lounge, where air from outside was pumped in to cool it, although the thinness did make some people faint. Luc wondered if airships would ever get the hang of balancing the atmosphere inside, which would allow for higher flight and faster travel.

He ensured he was alone, and made for a doorway at the side of the deck, which, according to the ship's schematics he'd found in the newspaper article on its maiden voyage, should lead to the cargo hold. Indeed it did, and he pulled a small phosphor lantern from his jacket pocket. When he flipped the switch, the internal chamber was flooded with a chemical that caused the microscopic animalcules to light up. He didn't know how the science worked, only that it did. A previous Marquis had possessed the curiosity for science and had made great strides in his long life, but as for Luc, he'd been only interested in art and pleasure. And aesthetics, which cloaked his current state in bitter irony.

Madame Kindred had been one of the last people on the

ship, so he hoped her crates had been loaded toward the top. He hadn't realized just how big the cargo hold was, but it made sense—the luggage and packages had to be stacked evenly so as to distribute their weight throughout the hold. It wouldn't do for the deck to tilt one way or the other. Everything was also strapped down. He admired whoever had come up with the system.

When he found the crates, he breathed a sigh of relief. The light from his hand lantern had started to dim, and he didn't want to use his spare quite yet. He pried the top off the first crate with a crowbar he'd found near the entrance and dug through the straw. None of the paintings or small statues spoke to him like the one in Madame's room had. He silently berated himself for having chosen the painting of the priestess in the temple over the child with the ball when he'd made that last fateful trip to Paris all those months ago. His great grandfather had been a man of subtlety, not obvious irony. Luc would have hidden the clues to the Monceau legacy in a painting like the one that had fooled him, counting on others to dismiss it for being too obvious. Not in a painting of a child with a ball.

After searching through both crates, he admitted to himself that Madame had the best candidate in her room. It must be the child, and the symbols on the ball more than mere decoration. Concern for her overtook his desire to find the painting. She'd looked terrible that morning. Well, as terrible as a good-looking woman could. He wouldn't call her beautiful—her nose sat just a tad too long and her eyes could be bigger—but she had character, and when she smiled, her face transformed, lovely in its genuineness.

Luc shook his head as he replaced the paintings and the straw, securing the lids as best he could. Since when did he care about genuineness and authenticity in women? He couldn't be himself with them, couldn't reveal the secret—that he was the same Marquis de Monceau their mothers and grandmothers had swooned over twenty, forty, sixty years ago. No one could know him, so he made no effort to know them.

But something about Madame Veronica Kindred had sparked an interest in him that no one else had. If he had to identify the moment, it must have been when she wielded the chamber pot against her attacker. None of the other women of his acquaintance except perhaps Madame Cinsault had demonstrated such spirit or ingenuity.

Right, Madame Cinsault. Daphne. While he enjoyed this pleasure cruise, she remained a prisoner on the pirate ship. He half-smiled with the thought that she'd have them all whipped into shape. He should have been concerned for her safety, but he knew Le Rouge wouldn't want to damage such a valuable bargaining chip. Meanwhile, Luc hoped she was driving the bastard nuts.

"What's so funny, Monsieur?"

Luc wheeled around and dropped his phosphorous hand lamp. It shattered at his feet, the light fading to nothing. Two men stood in front of him, their own hand lanterns shining upward, deepening the shadows of their faces. One of them was tall and wore red-tinted goggles. The other...

"Monsieur Firmin," Luc said. "What brings you down to this part of the ship?"

Firmin shrugged and replied, "I suspect it's the same thing that drew you down here." But he didn't elaborate. The last time Luc had seen him before his accident, they'd argued. Luc hadn't liked the direction of the archaeology school Firmin had been trying to run. Firmin hadn't appreciated his opinion. They'd almost come to blows. Luc found himself clenching his fists, ready to hit Firmin, but also in case he needed to defend himself against the man in the goggles.

"Where is it?" the strange man asked, his voice raspy.

"Where is what?"

"The painting. You know the one we mean."

Luc gestured to the crate behind him. "I assure you I don't, but you're welcome to look through the crates if you like." He stepped sideways, but they moved to block him.

"Your eye for art is legendary, Marquis," Firmin said. "And I know that your ancestors hid the key to a great treasure in your collection."

His words struck Luc like ice water, which seeped through his skin and into his chest. "I am not a Marquis. I'm a humble art dealer."

Firmin laughed. "Humble is not a word I've ever heard to describe you, Marquis. You think you can hide behind your eyepatch—is that even real?—and your scar, but I see you."

Luc now found himself wishing he wasn't being seen for himself and not his injuries. He forced his fists to unclench. "I assure you, I don't know what you mean." He looked at the tall man in the goggles, who stood with his arms crossed but didn't say anything. "Your friend is spouting nonsense."

"You're the Marquis de Monceau," the man intoned. "You're not fooling anyone." Again, something about his voice sounded off. Luc wanted to get a closer look at him but dared not approach him. He wondered if Madame's chamber pot assault had somehow damaged the man's larynx.

"How about this?" Firmin asked. "You don't say anything to the captain about having seen us down here, and I won't reveal who you are to Inspector Davidson or the others."

Luc pressed his lips together. The last thing he wanted was to be in debt to Firmin, but what choice did he have?

There's always a choice, m'lad, he recalled one of his great uncles saying as Luc had practiced his English with him. *But sometimes it's not the one you'd like.*

"Fine," Luc spat. "I'll keep your secret if you keep mine." Then he recognized he'd all but admitted to his identity. "But aren't you going to introduce me to your friend?"

"No." Firmin grinned. "He likes to keep his secrets, as do I.

Only know that he doesn't sleep, so you'll not be able to catch him unawares."

Luc recognized the raspiness in the man's tone—gears in a voice box. "He's an automaton."

"Yes. Hence why no one's been able to find him. He can hide silently for hours." Firmin grinned, the shadows of his cheekbones touching his eyes and giving him a sepulchral look. "And he has the strength of ten men."

"But not enough to defeat a woman with a chamberpot." Luc laughed. "Didn't take that into account with the design, did you?"

"I'm not the one who designed him," Firmin pressed his lips together, and Luc surmised that Firmin had said more than he meant to. He'd looked briefly into automatons—they'd make the ultimate servants who wouldn't ask questions—but hadn't made it too far. Something about their ability for silence and stillness disturbed him.

"Who did?" Luc marveled at the complexity and realism the creature presented.

"A talented tinkerer. No more questions, Marquis. Remember our deal—you don't tell anyone you saw me and my friend down here, and I won't reveal your secret. The new look suits you, by the way. You finally look the scoundrel you are."

Luc didn't thank him. The two men—well, man and machine—let him pass. As he ascended, he heard Firmin say to his metal companion, "All right, go ahead and take the top off. The Marquis is a good bluffer, so something could be in there."

"Bon chance, mes amis," Luc whispered, of course not meaning it. He knew where the true treasure lay. Now he had to figure out how to get it without alerting Firmin as to its value. He guessed that either Firmin or the automaton would be watching him once they satisfied their curiosity about the artwork in the crates.

Suddenly the airship felt much too small.

8

____

Henry Davidson watched Monsieur Firmin and the automaton unload all the art that the Marquis—yes, Henry indulged in a moment of pride when his guess had been confirmed—had just gone through. Whatever they all sought, it wasn't in there. Firmin re-packed the crate carefully, demonstrating his knowledge of how to store works of art. Too bad the man had the personality of a crook. He would have made a great addition to the art world in the newly re-United States. Not that it was unheard of for a criminal to escape the old world and reinvent himself in the new. Henry, although not a criminal, had entertained such thoughts for his own future. What would it be like, he wondered, to not be Inspector Davidson, but to just be Henry, with a wife and family and normal life?

But the only woman he could imagine himself with was not a normal woman.

He rubbed his leg, the barely healed injury making the muscles cramp after so long crouched behind some crates. He'd followed the Marquis down into the hold after seeing him disappear in a spot where no doors led from the passenger compartments to the deck, and he'd been lucky the other two men hadn't seen him. He doubted the automaton could see much, although the goggles could potentially give it information beyond what human eyes could provide. Henry recognized the advanced design, and he'd bet his favorite pair of gloves that Paul Farrell had been the maker. Could this be his lucky break and bring him one step closer to capturing the one criminal who'd escaped and stained his spotless career?

And how the hell had Firmin been able to afford an automaton? Was that what he'd done with the money he'd stolen from his students? But to what purpose?

More mysteries. Firmin and the automaton left the hold, and Henry finally straightened. He wiggled his toes to bring feeling back into his feet, and he clenched his toes as tingling turned into a wave of stabbing pins and needles. Once he could move comfortably, he investigated the crates that had been unpacked and repacked by Firmin and Monceau. The bills stuck into their side compartments told him that the crates belonged to Madame Kindred and were headed to Terminus via Charleston.

Interesting. He'd have to have a chat with Madame Kindred. And confirm for himself that Cloutier was indeed the marquis. He hadn't admitted it, although he had acquiesced to the blackmail. But even an accusation no one believed could be damning. That's why Henry needed to make doubly sure Cloutier and the Marquis were indeed the same person. False accusations cut both ways.

"AMATEUR. Everyone thinks they can draw. But so few can."

When Veronica returned to her cabin, she found the painting of the boy with the ball sitting on the bed. She could have sworn she'd put it back on the nightstand after looking at it that morning, seeing if the symbols had become any clearer. She'd at first been reluctant to do so—her nightmares had been strange and disturbing, of temple ceremonies and threads of lives twisting and elongating to a delicate, mad thinness that she couldn't explain. But what could a child with a ball have to do with such odd nocturnal visions? So, she'd picked him up, looked at the ball, and noted that the sun continued to bring out the symbols, now resembling curlicues more than smudges.

The child's face changed, too. Whereas the boy's eyes had seemed empty and flat before, now they had a certain ageless-ness to them, almost like someone had accidentally started to paint an adult's eyes but then had changed their mind. Veronica didn't know what that meant. Perhaps she should try to preserve the painting, keep it out of the sun. She'd tucked it back against the wall, where no sunbeam could find it unless the ship made an about-face turn.

So how had it moved to the bed? She wanted to believe she'd left it there, that perhaps she'd picked it up for one more look and had absentmindedly set it in the middle of the bright square of sunlight that made the white brocade duvet blaze. Right, the bed was made. Perhaps a maid had put the painting there, taken in by its charm.

Now irritation added to the tired itch around Veronica's eyes. How dare they touch her things? But on some level, she knew that no maid had moved the painting, although she might not want to admit it yet.

"The deranged thinking of a sleep-deprived mind," she muttered. She couldn't help but look at the child's face, so inno-cent and yet so wise. What was he thinking?

She should draw him.

The thought hit her full-force, and she dropped the painting back on the bed. She couldn't draw him. Couldn't draw anything, really. But then Monsieur Cloutier's words came back to her, his scoffing, *"Amateur. Everyone thinks they can draw. But so few can."* Well, it had been a while, but she was no amateur. She still remembered the little sparrow who had hopped on the bench she'd escaped to during yet another interminable teatime when the other girls talked about beaux and the gathering clouds of war. She'd known she wasn't supposed to draw—her uncle had forbidden it—but she couldn't help it. She'd torn a page out of her diary, and sketched the bird, his inquisitive expression and bright eyes coming to life on her page.

That sketch had been the one that Peter had found...

Well, no one would find whatever drawing she made today. She'd make sure to burn it. She propped the child—she couldn't think of him as a mere painting—on the writing desk and pulled out a sheet of paper, which she'd originally brought along to catch up on letter-writing. She found a pencil, took a deep breath, and loosely laid the point against the paper. Now she no longer saw the child, just shapes—ovals, circles, overlapping squares of shoulders and waist/legs.

She got a few faint lines on the page—not even enough to demonstrate what she tried to do—before her hand cramped. She hadn't realized she held the pencil that tightly. She stretched her fingers, loosened her grip, and tried again, but this time her hand shook too badly. The image of Peter, gaunt from illness and deprivation during the Siege of Charleston, flashed into her mind. "I'm sorry," his specter said. "I'm so sorry."

Veronica forced herself to look at the child and she thought she saw a hint of pity come into his eyes. "I bet you didn't have to deal with any of this," she snapped at him. She could recognize her irrationality, but anger bubbled up inside her, and she threw the pencil to the ground and buried her face in her hands. This time the anger cleansed and broke through the wall she'd built between her present self, the successful art critic and historian, and the past her, the girl who just wanted to draw.

For the first time since Peter died, she allowed herself to cry, really cry instead of weep. When her sobs subsided, she found the pencil and tried again, but the drawing wouldn't come. She sat there for hours, stubborn, waiting for the block to dissipate, but when the shadows turned long and the light golden, indicating the dinner hour approached, she laid the pencil on the desk with trembling hands.

The anger might have broken through her block and allowed her to grieve the girl she'd not been able to become, but she still lacked one thing—trust in herself and her ability both to draw and to love again. How the two had become so intermingled, she didn't want to think, to question, but they had.

She rose on shaky feet to dress for dinner. Before she left, she put the painting in a drawer.

HAUNTED. That was how Madame Kindred looked to Luc. This evening she wore a black gown edged in gold lace. The color was all wrong for her in spite of the obvious luxury of the dress. It made her paler, highlighted the shadows of tiredness on her face, and dulled her hair. Luc pictured Léonard Basquet paying for such extravagance with a shake of his head and a grin, imagining the pleasure he'd have taking it off...

No, Luc reminded himself, Madame had likely paid for it herself, had it made at a Parisian modiste. She liked beautiful things, he could tell. Times had changed. Women no longer needed men's help to look beautiful, to feel lovely.

But he wouldn't mind taking it off of her. She smiled as she spoke with the captain and some of the other passengers, but the dark circles under her eyes had deepened, and he caught a hint of red around the lids. Had she been crying?

He had to unclench his hands, which had gone into fists at

the thought of someone hurting her. Again, her life was none of his business. He needed to get the painting and get away. She wore the key to her chamber on a chain around her neck. His attempts to charm the maids into letting him close enough to "borrow" a key had failed. When had women gotten so assertive?

Or perhaps his appearance could be to blame. No longer the handsome Marquis de Monceau, now simply an art dealer with an eyepatch and a scar, he'd sunk to become another common man with ill intentions rather than a nobleman who could dangle a title in front of a desperate woman. Or play hard to get. Sometimes he liked being on the other side of the game, too. Had he relied on his title so much? His looks? He'd thought women saw something worthy in him, something interesting due to his long life and education, but perhaps not.

The realization stung every time it surfaced in his mind, and he took another sip of bourbon, his traditional favorite. It didn't matter who knew—that recklessness had come after the second glass. He felt on display, the ruined Marquis, although no one looked at him beyond the usual curious looks about his injuries. His deformities.

"Good evening, Monsieur."

Henry Davidson's voice at Luc's elbow made him jump. He turned to see Davidson standing there, a glass of champagne in hand. Whereas the others' glances had slid over him, the inspector's shrewdness had returned, and he seemed to study Luc. His eyes maintained their eagle focus over his pleasant smile, and Luc no longer found himself reckless about who recognized him. Indeed, the attention of Henry Davidson was sobering, and Luc felt sorry for any woman on the other end of it. He couldn't imagine the man being romantic. Such bitter irony that he'd now have more of a chance at it than Luc.

"Good evening, Inspector," Luc said, glancing around for a chance to escape the conversation.

"How are you enjoying the voyage?" The question sounded innocent enough, but Luc wondered if it had a second meaning. Could Davidson know what he'd been up to, sneaking into the hold and then trying to charm the maids? Davidson would have made a good priest, powerful in the confessional.

Luc hadn't been to confession in a decade. Confessing the same sins for a century had gotten old, so he'd stopped bothering.

"I find air travel to be enlightening," Luc—or maybe the bourbon—said. "You see sides of people and the world you'd never notice otherwise."

"Agreed." Henry sipped his champagne. "One never knows what someone will reveal when in a situation like this. Have you traveled much?"

Luc reached for the story he'd made up for Stephan Cloutier, but the details eluded him, mixing up his past and the one he'd made for his alter ego. "Here and there. You know how the job demands it."

Henry's smile faltered. "That I do."

Luc saw the wavering of Davidson's focus on him and decided to press the matter. "And have you traveled much?"

The mask of pleasantness returned. "That I have. And I've met many interesting people along the way. Criminals, mostly."

Luc shuddered. "That doesn't sound pleasant."

"It is when you get to uncover their secrets." Henry touched his lips to the glass, but Luc couldn't tell if the level of the liquid inside changed. "What about you, Monsieur? What secrets do you think we're surrounded by?"

Luc wanted to say, *"Too many to count,"* but he waited a beat too long, and someone joined them, a portly woman with enough jewelry to weigh down a dozen airships.

"Oh, Mister Davidson, *just* the man I wanted to see." She hooked her arm through Davidson's. "I've heard you're an *Inspector.* How *exciting.*"

Luc wondered if she'd emphasize one word in each of her sentences but didn't stick around to find out. He needed to see where Madame Kindred had gotten off to. He needed to get that painting from her room and then take an escape compartment back to France before they got too far from land. And if he had to seduce her to get into her room...

9

———

Veronica felt a warm presence behind her and looked up to see Monsieur Cloutier standing there. He held a glass of brown liquid that smelled sweet and alcoholic at the same time. She kept herself from wrinkling her nose. She wouldn't judge. Especially not since she'd grabbed a flute of champagne off a waiter's tray as soon as she'd reached the dining room and downed half the glass in one gulp. The burning steadied her, although she knew she'd have a headache later. Sparkling wine always did that to her—highlighted her regrets. She drank the rest of the glass much more slowly but didn't say no to a second one.

"I'm afraid I can't invite you to join me tonight," Captain Viero told them. "I have to entertain some dignitaries from Prussia." He sighed, and Veronica didn't envy him. He'd told them that they wanted to increase the luxury airlines' options and routes, which meant they'd have to go over enemy airspace. Part of the purpose of the journey was to make nice with Prussia, who had kicked France's derriere in the recent conflict. But, as Veronica knew, commercial interests overcame patriotism for many individuals. She'd seen it enough at home with her uncle trading with the Confederate supporters. Of course, if he hadn't, they'd have starved. France's people would, too, if they couldn't build their industries.

"I'm sure I can entertain Madame Kindred," Cloutier said, and Veronica did step away from him. How much had he drunk?

Viero didn't seem to notice. "I'm sure you can as well. I'll have a bottle or two of my finest wine sent over to you."

"You don't—" Veronica stopped and watched the captain walk away to greet a dark-haired man in military gear and a beautiful blonde woman who looked down her nose at everything.

"Well, shall we?" Cloutier asked. His lopsided smile high-lighted the redness in his cheeks.

"Does it hurt?" she blurted, then looked down, her own face heating.

"Does what hurt?" he asked and guided them to a table set for two in a sort of alcove where they'd only be visible from the front. Such an intimate space! Veronica drew back, but he was too strong for her, and she didn't want to make a scene. She'd make sure he didn't pull the curtain.

"Your face," she mumbled. How could she have been so inconsiderate? But as they settled into the alcove, she wondered what he was thinking.

He leaned back and rubbed his scar. "It does sometimes," he admitted in a tone she hadn't heard from him. Gentle. Quiet. And—she shivered—honest and vulnerable. "My scar doesn't like the dry air up here. Makes it pull worse."

She thought about saying, *"I'm sorry"* but knew it would be useless. There was no amount of sorry that could restore what he'd lost. She couldn't imagine trying to make it through life with only one eye. Would she be less able to appreciate art without the perception of depth?

"But that's what champagne is for," he said. Thankfully the

waiter had whisked away his half-finished bourbon, but they'd brought two flutes and poured from a bottle Veronica recognized as the vintage Viero only served at his table.

"To new friends," Cloutier said, and Veronica had to clink his glass and drink from her own. The taste turned sour in her mouth, and she welcomed the first course—some sort of creamy soup—to help cut it. No matter how much she tried to eat, she couldn't get ahead of the wine, which kept coming. Soon her head felt light, and she found herself laughing at something Cloutier said about the Prussian man's mustache.

"What part of France are you from, Monsieur?" She looked up at him and noted the pained look on his face. "Or you don't have to answer if you don't like. I just realized I know very little about you, and I've been prattling on the past couple of times we've been together." She gestured to her almost empty glass of Burgundy. "It's the wine. It makes me talkative."

"I'm from not too far outside of Paris," he said, then he gave her another half-smile. "A small village, nothing important. But there is an interesting legend in the area."

"Oh?" She leaned toward him, decided the distance was too personal, leaned back, and ended up relying on the cushions on the chair to keep her upright. "Whoopsie."

He helped her to right herself. "Yes. Legend has it that the man in the castle isn't the great-great-great-great grandson of the man who built it, but rather merely the grandson."

"That would make him really old." She blinked, but the room kept swimming.

"Yes, it would. That's why it's a legend."

"What happened?" She dug back through her limited knowledge of fairy tales. "Did he make a deal with a wizard or something?"

"The legend says that the old Mar—er, Duke did a favor for a powerful wizard, and when asked what he wanted in return, wished for a long life so he could enjoy his riches. But the wizard didn't like granting such a large wish and instead cursed him and his descendants. You see, he did as the Duke asked, but in excess. He lived to grow his wealth, to delight in it, but then he discovered the price of his wish. As did his son, and his son. They keep their youthful looks for decades, but everyone they love dies, and they eventually have to go into hiding and pretend to be their own sons, returned from traveling abroad. They have to act as though they're something they're not for most of their lives, which kills their souls and their ability to enjoy anything."

Veronica nodded. "That's tough. I know how that feels."

"Oh, do you?" Cloutier practically sneered, but Veronica didn't take offense.

"Once upon a time," she said, "a young girl loved to draw more than anything else. She'd inherited the talent from her father, but he and the girl's mother had died in a typh—er—plague, leaving her to live with her uncle's family. He forbade her from drawing so she could grow up and become a teacher and attract a husband with her *practical* skills. He lied to her and told her she had no talent." Warm tears trickled down her face. "Then he made her husband promise to do the same. By the time she found out about the ruse..." She shook her head. "It doesn't matter. I'm sorry, Monsieur, your tale was fascinating."

He looked at her with an odd expression. "As was yours. You may finish if you like."

"There is only one way to finish—it was too late." She tried to shrug, but she knew she didn't pull it off. "I'm sorry. I need to return to my chamber. It's stuffy in here, and my head aches."

"I'll escort you."

She wanted to protest, but everyone on the ship thought they were sleeping together anyway, so what did it matter? She'd probably be horrified at herself in the morning for allowing it, but right now the wine wrapped her brain in a lovely fog divorced from planning or consequences. He kept his hand at the small of her back, and his warmth anchored her and steadied her. Did the ship lurch, or was it her? She couldn't tell. She almost giggled, but something pressed in on her, told her to be quiet.

"Madame, did you lock the door when you left your room?" Cloutier asked in a whisper.

"Of course." She dug the key on its chain from her bodice. It sparkled when she held it up.

"Then it appears as though someone has broken into your room."

THE SMALL SOUND, a tiny scuffle easily lost in the constant hum of the ship, could have easily been lost, but it sobered Luc. The bourbon and champagne and Burgundy—good gods, how much had he drunk?—tried to replace the curtain they'd put over his brain, but he mentally brushed them away. That was one of the odd talents he'd inherited from his ancestors—alcohol didn't affect him unless he wanted it to, and he could make the effects go away when he needed, although he might still pay with a hangover on the morrow.

Veronica swayed on his arm but didn't say anything. In the dim light, he could barely see her blinking, attempting to clear her brain, but he knew she wouldn't be able to. What to do with her? He didn't want her to get hurt, but he didn't have time to spirit her away. A certain feeling, a gathering of power from the edges of the corridor, told him things were about to get ugly.

They hadn't moved since Luc had spoken, and he leaned to her ear and whispered, "Stay here."

She nodded. "Be careful," she whispered back. He almost scoffed, but he didn't. He'd never been known to be careful, at least not when he'd been the Marquis de Monceau. But he'd changed in that, as in so many ways, so he squeezed her hand.

He crept forward until he could clearly see the door to her chamber, which stood slightly ajar. A sliver of moonlight spilled into the hallway, and he suspected that whoever was in there hadn't intended to leave the door open. But when one dealt with the Legacy, one's wishes didn't always—*ever*—matter. The light waxed and waned too subtly for most humans' eyes to notice, but Luc saw. He'd been right about the painting, and Great-Grandfather Monceau—or whatever spirit inhabited the painting—was angry.

He peered into the room and saw two figures in there—Firmin and the automaton. Whereas the false man had looked normal in the light of the phosphorous lamps, the moonlight illuminated the fine weave of his skin and gave it an eerie luminosity, especially with the glowing red goggles. Firmin also wore goggles, presumably to help his vision in the dark. Luc didn't need any help. The Legacy had given him excellent night vision. It had helped him to survive on many other tricky occasions, and he hoped he wouldn't have any trouble now.

"It has to be in here somewhere," Firmin muttered as he dug through the desk drawers. "I know the woman has it."

"Small painting," the automaton intoned as though repeating instructions to itself. It yanked the duvet cover off the bed and did the same with the sheets. It then lifted the mattress like it weighed nothing.

Firmin had emptied the dresser drawers, and Luc tried not to look at the lacy underthings scattered around the floor like downed ghosts. The drawers had been pulled from the desk, their contents similarly scattered. Now that he recognized the painting, he could feel it in there somewhere. The automaton reached under the bed, stretching its long arm all the way back, and pulled something out.

"Small painting," it said again and held it out to Firmin, who took it. He lifted it up to where it caught the moonlight, and the symbols on the ball glowed, as did the child's eyes.

"This must be it," Firmin said. "I recognize the symbols. They were also in that manuscript that that English chit stole from me in Paris."

Luc raised his eyebrows. What manuscript? Right, Firmin had gone to the police after the siege had lifted and complained that one of his students, Iris McTavish, had stolen an ancient manuscript from him. The scandal of the school had come out soon after, and Firmin had dropped the charges, desiring to stay as far away from the law as possible, or so Luc had heard. Could that ancient document hold clues to his legacy? He'd have to see if Henry Davidson could give him an introduction, assuming Luc could keep up his charade.

The light around the edges of the room dimmed, and Luc braced himself. He had been about to confront the two thieves, but even with his extra strength, he knew he'd be no match for the automaton. So he decided to let the scene play out. He glanced behind him and bit his tongue over an exclamation of surprise when he found Veronica beside him, peering around him.

"They have the painting," she mouthed.

He nodded. "Get back," he warned, but she didn't move. Nor could he. He knew they shouldn't watch, shouldn't witness what was about to happen, but the Legacy, once revealed, liked to show off its power. His grandfather had explained it to him as more than an inherited energy or ability. It could be a guardian spirit—or a vengeful one. Few had seen it since the original conferring of it upon their ancestor along with their excessive longevity, and when they had, they'd been content to leave it in whatever object it desired to stay in. Spirits were capricious, after all.

The picture's glow intensified, and the room grew darker and darker. Veronica covered her eyes against the brightness, and Luc squinted. Although no air moved, something stirred his hair and clothing.

Firmin stood, seemingly frozen, his mouth working and his eyes wide. The silver-white glow around the picture darkened to blood red, and Firmin arched backward as it enveloped him. He screamed, and the automaton stiffened and made a gurgling sound. Luc pulled Veronica to him, making sure her face remained pressed to his chest so she wouldn't see. But he couldn't look away. Firmin's cry faded, and he slumped to the floor, dropping the painting, which floated to sit on the top of the desk. The room went dark for an instant, then resumed its moonlit brightness. All was as it had been—no scattered papers, no torn garments, no destroyed inkwells. Just two figures lying on the floor.

"What happened?"

Luc allowed Veronica to pull away, but she swayed, so he didn't let her go completely. She gasped. "The room. It's back as it was. But who are they?"

Luc made sure she could stand and then crossed the floor and pressed two fingers to Firmin's neck. Nothing, as he expected. "Did you ever hear of a Monsieur Firmin, formerly with the Louvre?"

"Yes." She frowned. "He lost his position over some scandal."

A suspicion tickled the back of Luc's brain. "He lost a lot more, and I wonder who hired him to grab the painting."

"Monsieur, I'm feeling faint again."

He caught her against him before she crumpled to the ground.

THE PAINTING HAD KILLED two men. The thought wedged in Veronica's brain and wouldn't allow her to completely lose consciousness. She couldn't look away from the slumped figures on the floor. How was that possible? How had it returned her room to its non-torn-up state and how could it just lie there on the bed, looking innocent?

A painting. She was thinking about a painting like it was a person, or a...being? Living thing?

She swallowed against the thick acid liquid that clogged her throat. She couldn't throw up now. She'd have to pass by the bodies to get to the water closet. Hell, she could barely walk. Her knees seemed to be debating whether to hold her up or not.

"Are you all right?" Cloutier asked.

Veronica looked up at him and realized she'd been holding on to him, still half-tucked against him. She released his clothing and stepped back, then forward again when she recognized that away meant toward the murdered men and the painting.

"No, I'm not all right," she said, her voice weak instead of the strength she needed it to have. He moved aside to let her into the hallway, and the distinctly cooler air brushed her cheeks and helped her to breathe. Several swallows—and not looking at the mess in her room—brought her stomach under control.

"Here," he said. He gave her a cup of water. She recognized the cup as coming from the table in her room, where a water pitcher had been set in a tray with indentations in the bottom that kept things from sliding around. She almost knocked it aside—she didn't want anything from that room anymore, but dropped her hand, her fist clenched.

"You need to drink this," he insisted. "It's only water. But you've had a shock, and you need to drink something."

His words made no sense, and her hand shook too much to take the cup, so he guided the cup to her lips and helped her to drink. The water settled her stomach but not the tight squeeze in her chest.

"What... What was that?" she finally asked. If she knew what she'd seen, perhaps she could make sense of it.

"It was the Legacy of Monceau." His tone had taken on a grim quality. "It does not appreciate being interfered with."

"So why didn't it...?" She couldn't finish the sentence, but he apparently knew what she tried to say.

"Why didn't it hurt you? I don't know."

She looked up at him. "That's not comforting." Then, in an almost whisper, "What is it? The Legacy, exactly, I mean?" She needed some sort of explanation, something to help her make sense of it.

He ran a hand through his hair. "I can't explain it, only that it's something that we—I mean the Marquis of Monceau—was charged to take care of and guard."

She caught his slip. He knew she'd caught it. Suddenly things clicked into place, and anger flashed through her. He'd lied to her. Men always lied to her. "You're the Marquis," she said, stabbing his chest with her finger. "You were the man there at the chateau. You saved me from the pirates. And then from the automaton." He'd saved her. She couldn't be angry, then, could she?

"You were doing a damned fine job saving yourself," he said, catching her finger and holding her hand to his chest. "I simply helped some."

"Yes, I was, wasn't I? And what were you doing there?"

"Looking for the painting. I'd been...stupid." He sighed and looked away. "I only saw what was on the surface, and it got me into trouble." He gestured to his face. "It got me this."

Veronica's feelings swung back and forth from anger—he'd lied to her—to gratitude—he'd saved her—to sympathy— whatever she'd gone through, she had come out stronger. And not marked, at least not physically. They'd both lost a lot.

She put her other hand to his cheek, feeling the stubble along his chin. He didn't move away, but he didn't lean into her caress, either. Instead he watched her warily. She wanted to say something, but the hardness around his mouth and the pain in his undamaged eye dared her to not fall into platitudes, false reassurances. So instead she kissed him.

He stiffened, and she tried to draw back—what had she been thinking?—but he pressed his hand to the back of her head and kept her lips on his, which opened. She hadn't been kissed since Peter, but any thought of him merely flitted through her awareness. Cloutier claimed her with his tongue, one hand still holding hers between their chests, the other pressed against the small of her back.

A rustling sound made them break apart, and they stepped to opposite sides of the hall as one of the maids came through.

"Would you like me to turn down your bed, Miss?" she asked, no sign of shock at the improper behavior she'd witnessed.

The recollection of the two bodies on the floor of the room slammed into Veronica's brain. "No, no thank you. In fact, would you fetch Inspector Davidson?"

The man she'd known as Stefan Cloutier started to protest, then stopped. With a sigh, he said, "I suppose we'd have to bring him into it eventually."

The maid scurried off, and Veronica held out her hands. "No, stay away. I can't kiss you again." Even if she wanted to. "I don't even know your real name."

He paused for so long she thought he wouldn't tell her, but then said, "Luc de Moncels, former Marquis of Monceau, at your service."

10

The dining room had gotten stuffy with the scent of heavy perfume and sweaty bodies even though the bulk of the dinner crowd had cleared out. Henry didn't know what was wrong with the airship's ventilation system, but he hoped Viero had his best engineers on it. He finally made it to the outer deck, where the bracing air cleared away the fog from his brain and odors from his nose. He wasn't accustomed to drinking so much wine.

A flash of light caught his peripheral vision, and he turned to see the windows from the upper deck of the first-class cabins were dark except for one. At first, he thought someone moved about with a candle, but then he recognized the phosphorescent light from the torches like the Marquis and Monsieur Firmin had in the hold. A quick mental trip through the upper deck's schematics confirmed his suspicion—someone was searching Madame Kindred's room.

A brighter flash of light and the sensation of something shifting, although he couldn't discern anything moving, caused him to make his way toward the upper deck. A breathless maid met him on the stairs.

"Oh, Monsieur Davidson, I'm glad it's you. Madame Kindred asked me to fetch you."

Right, he'd seen her leave with the Marquis. He'd wondered at them being so obvious, but the longer the voyage had gone on, the more social restrictions had unraveled, and hardly anyone batted an eye at them. Or perhaps Viero, in an effort to stop complaints, had been too generous with the ship's wine.

If she'd sent for him, then she must be unhurt. Or so he hoped.

He found Madame Kindred and "Monsieur Cloutier" standing outside her room. She looked pale but composed, and he scowled. Henry wondered what had interrupted their lovers' tryst, or if there had been one.

"You summoned me?" he asked.

"That was fast," Cloutier said.

"I was heading up this way. I saw light in Madame's window." Henry wouldn't let the man intimidate him.

"There were—are—two men in my cabin," she said and swallowed. Nausea?

"What happened?" Henry thought it was a simple question, but the two of them looked at each other.

A sound like a child's giggle made the hairs on the back of his neck raise, and Madame clutched Cloutier's arm.

"Did you hear that?" she asked.

Cloutier and Henry both nodded. They peered through the door, and Henry saw the room, neatly made up, and two figures slumped on the floor. He rushed in, bending to check the first one's pulse. He didn't have one, and Henry recognized the other one as the automaton. What could have felled him? Then he saw the painting on the bed.

He first noticed the ball the child held, specifically the symbols. In his study of arcane and secret societies, he'd come across such things, and these symbols looked much like the ones on a ring in the custody of Iris McTavish Bailey, a premier amateur archaeologist. She said it had taken her consciousness into a far distant past, and he'd believed her, especially after the events in Boston. He reached for the painting, but Cloutier stopped him.

"Don't make the mistake they did." He inclined his head to the dead man and automaton. "It didn't like being interfered with."

"So you can touch it, as can Madame?" The situation grew more interesting by the second.

"Yes," Cloutier picked it up and made as though he would hand it to Madame. She backed away.

"I have no desire to touch the thing. It just killed someone."

Henry didn't blame her, especially as she apparently still fought the shock and horror of what she'd just witnessed. He'd seen enough death in his career that, while he never disrespected the dead, he admitted to a certain amount of hardening around it. Seeing her distress made him wonder what kind of man he'd become that he could react so coolly to a murderous painting. Or, more specifically, a vengeful spirit of some sort.

Then it clicked. That's why his organization had been so interested in the Marquis. "It's the Legacy, isn't it?" Henry asked. "The Legacy of Monceau."

Cloutier swallowed and placed the painting on the bed.

"That's how you're able to touch it. It's good to see you again, Marquis. We all thought you were dead."

Cloutier crossed his arms. "The man you knew as the Marquis is dead, Inspector. An accused traitor cannot claim his title, his lands. Do you know who set me up?"

Henry shook his head. "No, only that some very powerful people were unhappy with your decision to leave Paris. You had —have—many enemies."

"Not if they don't know I'm alive."

Henry realized that Madame didn't seem surprised by the revelation of the Marquis' identity. "She knows?"

"He just told me," she murmured. "He rescued me at the chateau."

"She rescued herself," Cloutier insisted. "I merely helped distract the...pirates."

"You have changed." The old Marquis would never have given credit to a woman but would rather have hogged the glory for himself. "And what about the pirates?"

"They're after this, and if Firmin knew about it, others may as well. Hell, he may have been sent by them. Le Rouge has many layers of backup planning."

Henry nodded. "And what would be the final plan if they knew Firmin was dead, his automaton disabled, and you weren't cooperative?"

Cloutier responded without hesitation. "They'd attack the ship."

"Then we have to keep this a secret. We don't know who among the crew is aligned with them." Henry rubbed his temples with the thumb and forefinger of his right hand. "But we can't leave the bodies here. We'll have to dispose of them somehow." And he would have to explain something to Viero.

A shadow loomed in the doorway, and a new voice said, "That won't be necessary. Men, tie up the Inspector. He won't be needed."

Pirates! Veronica had never seen pirates before, but the two large burly men in the doorway wore enough weapons to arm a small battalion, had piercings and tattoos, and interspersed among the ink were the scars to show they'd seen their fair share of battles. But most of all, they had an air of ruthlessness about them.

As for the third, who'd spoken with a cultured British

accent, he also had a dangerous air, but he lacked weapons, markings, or piercings.

"Matthew, I didn't think Le Rouge let you off the ship more than once a year," the man Veronica still thought of as Stephan Cloutier said. *Marquis*, she reminded herself, although that wasn't going to be helpful here. And he knew them? At least one of them. Yet another secret. Damn her traitorous heart, how could she be attracted to a man who hid so much?

A motion by her foot made her look downward. The man—automaton's?—fingers twitched.

"He does if it's to fetch something he really wants, and he knows I'll return. You know he has us all by the nuts. Pardon, ma'am." He ducked his head to Veronica.

Veronica raised her eyebrows. An apologizing pirate? And one who blackmailed. She supposed she should be relieved, perhaps, that this pirate did take prisoners. But then what?

Cloutier and the man continued to trade barbs, and Veronica, who stood closest to the automaton, noticed tiny movements. How could she use it to her advantage?

Inspector Davidson nudged her and spoke softly. "When it wakes, it will be disoriented. Don't think—just use the distraction to get out of here."

"What about you?"

"I'll be right behind you."

The two burly pirates moved toward them, and one of them grabbed Cloutier. The other one reached for her, but she ducked, and she gave the automaton a swift kick to the side. It let out a loud groan, and everyone froze.

"Small painting," it moaned and struggled to its feet. The pirate who didn't have Cloutier pulled out a knife and crouched in a fighting stance. Veronica tried to do as Davidson had said, but Matthew grabbed her arm.

"Oh, no you don't, Mrs. Kindred. Le Rouge wants you, too."

She stomped on his foot and cursed—he wore reinforced

shoes, which withstood her dinner slipper. She hissed against the pain that radiated up from her foot.

Davidson dodged the weaving automaton and the pirate, who'd gotten trapped between it and the lavatory door. Matthew made to trip him, but Davidson pivoted and elbowed him on the side of the face. Matthew didn't go down, though. Instead, his grip tightened on Veronica's arm to the point she squeaked. She struggled, but he wouldn't let go, no matter how hard Davidson pulled. Matthew tugged her against him and held a knife to her throat.

"Give it up, Mister, or she gets it."

"I won't let them take you," Davidson promised, then darted out. Hopefully to get reinforcements.

The pirate and the automaton continued their odd dance, the pirate feinting and the automaton blocking. The metal man didn't seem interested in offensive moves, only defensive ones.

"Get the painting," Matthew said, "and let's get out of here."

The pirate who'd been fighting the automaton grabbed the picture. Veronica held her breath, waiting for the spirit to kill him, too, but nothing happened. He ducked under the automaton's arm, and rushed past them. Matthew strong-armed Veronica and the third man marched Cloutier out.

Instead of going to the main deck, they ascended to the roof of the passenger compartments, and Veronica saw a small craft nestled between the main balloon and the roof. It had a small balloon and propellers, and a tiny gondola, into which they were forced.

Veronica and Cloutier's wrists were tied, as were their ankles. They sat backward, and Matthew took the helm. The two muscular pirates perched on what looked like bicycle seats and started pedaling. The one who'd grabbed the painting had put it on the seat by Matthew, but when they took off, the gondola tilted, and it slid off and landed by Veronica's feet.

"Don't touch it," Matthew said.

Veronica gave him her brightest smile. Once they'd cleared the airship and the halo of warm air around it, she looked down to see the blackness of the ocean. She couldn't find the horizon—everything looked black around them except the *Acadia Pearl*, which grew smaller and smaller.

Anger bubbled up in her, bringing back the outrage of long ago, when her uncle and husband had determined the course of her life for her, or tried to. And now these men had stolen her away against her will. How dare they? How. Dare. They?

She reached down, struggling against the tightness of her corset and picked up the picture.

"What are you doing?" Matthew asked, his voice sharp with panic.

"What needs to be done. Take me back this minute or he goes overboard."

The two men who were pedaling stopped and looked at her in shock. She didn't have time to relish the fact that they finally saw her. The sickening sense of dropping accompanied the feeling of Veronica's butt leaving the seat.

"Keep pedaling, you imbeciles," Matthew screeched. They did, and the pressure of the bench reassured Veronica that they had stopped falling. "We're not going back," he said. He left the helm and made his way forward. "Give it to me."

"No."

"Veronica, what are you thinking?" Cloutier asked.

"I'm not going to go to the pirate ship. I refuse to be a prisoner."

"You don't have a choice," Matthew said. He reached out. "Now, Madame, the picture."

Veronica threw it at his head, but it missed. It spun, picking up impossible height, until it went over the back of the small airship.

Pain bloomed along Veronica's jaw when Matthew hit her.

"You stupid bitch, how could you?"

Hands around her neck choked her until she heard a grunt and opened her eyes to see Cloutier had managed to get Matthew off her. She took big, ragged gasps.

"Nicely done," Matthew said. "You just threw away your only bargaining chip."

Veronica wanted to kill him, but she only smiled. "Or was it yours?"

WHEN HENRY RETURNED to the room, he only found Firmin's body still there and a trail of blood droplets into the hall, where it disappeared. He instructed two of the men to take care of the body, then led the others in a search. A draft alerted him to the open door at the top of the stairs to the roof, and he saw scratch marks where the pirates' craft had been anchored. How had they evaded the guards on the deck? When he went down to check, he found the two guards snoozing, their heads on their chests, an empty bottle of rum and a pack of cards on the small table between them. He almost woke them to berate them, then smelled the bottle. A chemical odor alerted him to the fact that it had been tampered with. But by whom?

He steeled himself. He would have to go to Viero and admit failure. And that air pirates had taken two of his passengers and a valuable piece of artwork.

But that wasn't typical air pirate style. Henry considered this. He'd heard of Le Rouge, of course, the blackmailing pirate, but why not raid the ship and take everything of value they could? Especially with a traitor on board? No, they were waiting for something, but what?

Henry found Viero in his office, the dining room having since emptied out. Viero sat with a bottle of bourbon beside him, two fingers in a glass. At first he seemed to be asleep, but Henry noticed the stillness of his chest. Two fingers to his neck confirmed that the captain was barely alive, and a sniff at the bourbon told him from what.

"So the pirates are sewing chaos before they attack." He knew the tactic—cut off the head of an organization and then take advantage of the confusion. They likely thought Viero wouldn't be discovered until the morning.

A change in the pressure of the air behind him made Henry wheel about and grab whoever tried to sneak up on him by the neck. The cabin boy he'd seen earlier dropped the tray he'd been carrying and clutched at Henry's hand. Milky coffee spilled on Henry's shoes and splashed his pants. Henry sighed and let go.

"I'm sorry," he said. "What are you doing here?"

"My unc—er—the captain likes a cappuccino before bed," the boy said once he could get his breath. "Now I'll have to make it again."

"Did you bring this to him every night? And what did you almost say—the captain is your uncle?"

The boy nodded. "Yes, but he didn't like anyone to know. Either about the late coffee or me being his nephew. He fusses at me if I try to come to him during the day."

Henry's heart twisted. He hated this part of what he did. "Your uncle is almost dead."

"What? No!" The boy tried to dart around Henry, but it wasn't hard to hold him back.

"Yes. Do you know where the ship's doctor is?"

The child looked around, his eyes shining. "Yes. But I need to tell you—I saw something strange. A man who didn't move like a man."

The automaton? "Where?"

"In the hold. It's the shortcut I take from the kitchens to here." His face crumpled, but he held in his tears except for a quick wipe of his eyes.

"Thank you for telling me. Now go get the doctor as quickly as you can."

The boy nodded. "Yes, sir." He ran off.

"Good lad." Henry went down to the hold. At least the automaton hadn't gotten to the Pégase.

The trail of blood started again, and he heard cursing. He followed the sound to a spot on the wall and knelt. Yes, blood there, too.

Could the automaton have not been an automaton? If so, how had it survived whatever had killed Firmin? Henry had seen stranger. And if Firmin had been holding the painting, whatever it had emanated had likely been attenuated whenever it went to the automaton.

A hum alerted Henry, just the barest addition of sound to the constant thrum of the airship engine, and he leaped back. The automaton emerged, and it moved like a man. In fact, it had on the same clothing, but rather than being covered in fine linen and a wig, the head belonged to a young man with a scar across his face and a scowl. He carried the automaton head under one arm. Henry waited until it had passed him, then drew his weapon.

"I wouldn't go any farther if I were you," he said. "I have a gun."

The man held up his hands, but instead of turning slowly, dropped the head, spun around and rushed at him. Time stretched into slow motion. Henry fired, and the bullet bounced off the man's metal casing. He only had time for one more shot, and he knew what would happen if the man got to him. He fired at his face, and the man's head jerked back. Henry stepped out of the way of the body's fall.

Henry took a deep, shuddering breath. He hated killing, even in self-defense. When he examined the body, he found what looked like aether burn on the man's hands, which had been hidden by gloves, and a gash on one leg where the pirate's knife must have made contact.

Damn, he couldn't question him. In the man's bag, he found a bottle that smelled the same as the odd additional smell to the guards' rum and the captain's bourbon. Had he been planning to poison the whole ship?

A quick check of the Pégase revealed that it hadn't been tampered with, as far as Henry could tell. Now he'd have to hope Viero survived.

When he climbed to the office, he found Viero watching him.

"I have regrets," Viero told him. "Many many regrets."

"Don't talk," Henry said. "You've been poisoned. The doctor will be here soon."

Viero shook his head. "It's the pirates. They'll be back. They want La Pégase after she does what she wants with the painting."

"How do you know?" Then Henry almost smacked his head when the realization hit him. "You were the one in contact with them, weren't you? You and Firmin were working together."

Viero nodded. "Firmin turned on me," he rasped out.

"And you told me to look for someone on the inside to deflect attention from yourself." Henry rubbed his temples. How had he not looked for the double cross? Because he knew Viero. Or thought he did.

"Take La Pégase," Viero told him. "Find them. Help them. Then get help. We'll need reinforcements when the pirates attack."

And what would they do then? First things first. Henry didn't care what he'd have to do—he would get the Marquis and Madame Kindred back alive.

11

She'd thrown the painting. Luc couldn't believe she'd tossed it overboard. But he couldn't deny the evidence of his eyes—the slight course correction it had made that had lifted its trajectory and taken it out of the ship. Had wanted to escape? Regardless, it likely lay at the bottom of the ocean or had been torn apart by the waves.

Could its loss be for the better? It wouldn't hurt anyone. He'd acted callous about the deaths of Firmin and the automaton—if mechanical men could die—but seeing them had shaken him. It reminded him that the Legacy of Monceau came with a price. Could he be responsible for its actions? For losing track of the painting?

Of the two prisoners in the small airship, he couldn't help but feel that Madame Kindred was the stronger.

So of course the pirates had taken him to the stateroom that Le Rouge called his office and had brought Veronica to the brig. He'd wanted to go with her, to ensure her safety, but they'd torn him away from her. He still wasn't sure whether he'd fought to stay with her for her sake or his.

They'd left his hands tied, although his feet had been

unbound so he could walk. He sat on a stool and leaned against the wall. This wasn't how he'd intended this trip to go. But then, did life ever go how one expected? And now he'd finally get to meet the infamous Le Rouge, the pirate they all feared and hated. The man whose influence could be felt across the globe.

The last person Luc expected walked in. Daphne. She wore a long red dress, and her blonde hair had been done in an intricately braided style. She looked him over with her cool green eyes and said, "You look like hell, Luc."

Hearing his given name again shocked him into saying, "What are you doing here?"

She gestured around them. "This is my office. What do you think? A bit masculine for my taste, but one must keep up appearances."

"A bit..." His thoughts whirred like one of those little clockwork spy butterflies, barely landing on one idea before flitting to the next. He'd seen signs that she was more than she seemed. She'd shot a horseman who was pursuing them in Paris. She'd shown no fear when told she was to be taken to Le Rouge alone. She'd appeared and disappeared from his side with more freedom than a prisoner on a pirate ship should have.

"You're Le Rouge. La Rouge, rather."

She inclined her head, her lips curled in a secret smile he'd formerly found alluring. "I'm surprised it took you so long to catch on, but I'm glad you finally did." Her bosom heaved with a sigh. "Secrets are so exhausting."

"Was your late husband the original Le Rouge?" Luc asked. He couldn't imagine the diffident Monsieur Cinsault as a pirate, but he'd had a big enough shipping empire.

"No, but he knew." She shrugged.

"The whole time?" Monsieur Cinsault, for his liberal views on marriage, had seemed to be a law-abiding man in other respects.

"No." Now her expression tightened, deepening the lines

beside her mouth. "And when he found out, he tried to use it against me."

"So you had him stabbed in the back."

Her eyes glittered coldly. "I had him taken out of my way."

Luc couldn't believe what he heard. But then, he also could believe it.

"The attack on the airship outside of Paris—you orchestrated it."

"I needed to return to my ship. I needed to remain anonymous." She spread her hands. "I'm sorry for what happened to you. I truly didn't mean for you to be hurt so badly."

"So why didn't you tell me before now?"

She scoffed. "As if your life isn't wrapped in layers of secrets, Luc. And I needed to control you. You're so damn chivalrous. I know you wouldn't do anything that could get me hurt." She leaned forward over the desk. "Just as I've heard you wouldn't do anything that could result in harm to Mrs. Kindred. What is it with you and widows?"

He didn't say anything, but he felt the vise closing around his heart. She'd never release him. "You can't keep her prisoner here."

"Oh, I don't want to keep her." She waved one hand dismissively. "I want her to draw the painting she threw overboard. I looked into her when Basquet tapped her as his protégée. She used to be quite the artist when she was younger."

Luc recalled the story she'd told him. What had happened to make her stop drawing?

"You think she can reproduce the painting?"

"She'll have to. Careless of Matthew to allow the Legacy of Monceau to slip out of his hands like that. You, too."

"I was tied up."

"And not in a fun way. More's the pity." Her expression snapped back to seriousness. "I'm not jesting, Luc. I want her to recreate what she lost for me. If not, I'll throw her overboard to join it."

"And if she does, then what?"

Daphne grinned. "I'll keep her here to make sure you stay cooperative. It will be nice to have another woman on board."

Luc saw there was no way out, but he had to ask, "What do you want the Legacy for?"

"I know you're older than you claim." She steepled her fingers and looked at him with disturbing intensity. "And I know the legacy of Monceau has something to do with immortality, although that could be figurative."

"You want the spell." He shook his head. "It's more curse than blessing, Daphne."

She appeared to ignore him. "You think I don't see how you look at me differently? How your eye flicks to the lines by my mouth, the creases at the corners of my eyes? And then you look away an instant sooner than you used to, as do other men."

He could argue with her, but he'd lived long enough to recognize a person in the thrall of their own story.

She continued, the words rushing out of her. "Beauty is power, Luc. Especially for women." She clenched her fists. "Why do you think I hide here behind the specter of Le Rouge? So I don't have to rely on my looks to get what I want. But I will be found out eventually. And what then?"

"You'll still have everyone's secrets."

"Yes, but I will be a hunted woman. I need my looks to charm my way out of difficult situations."

Luc had thought similarly, and it had taken a scar and a lost eye to make him realize just how connected beauty and power could be. And how both could be meaningless in the end without one's freedom. It sounded like Daphne recognized the trap closing in on her as well. But he sensed she withheld something from him. She'd told one truth—she used distraction well. He'd have to bide his time to find out what she really wanted.

He forced himself to smile. "I'll do my best to convince her, but she's stubborn." He shrugged. "I like strong women."

"Oh, I'm aware. But if she doesn't cooperate, I'll have both of you thrown overboard."

THE TWO PIRATES who had strong-armed Luc into Daphne's study handled him less gently when they brought him back to a cell in the hold. With it being nighttime, he couldn't see much, but he heard someone else in there.

"Veronica, is that you?"

"Stephan... Luc?"

He hated that he'd lied to her, even though it had been necessary. "Yes, it's Luc."

He felt her rush to him and put her arms around him. "I was afraid he'd have you killed."

He laughed, thankful she couldn't see the play of expressions on his face. He could barely believe it. "He's not what I expected." He didn't know how else to say it. "He's a she. Daphne Cinsault. The woman who got me into this mess."

"What?" He felt her pull away and imagined her looking up at him with her golden eyes. The longer he stayed in there, the more his eyesight adjusted, and he could now make out dim shapes.

"Yes, she lied to me all along. But she wants you to do something. She wants you to recreate the painting."

She went still. "I...can't."

He recalled their conversation at dinner, which had only been a few hours previously but felt like weeks ago. "That fairy tale you told me. That was you, wasn't it? The girl who couldn't draw?"

She nodded, and something wet fell on his hands. He wanted to wipe away her tears, but he didn't want to hurt her.

"What happened?" he asked. "Truly? To make you stop drawing."

She released his hands and walked away. "I can't talk about it. It's too painful."

"Would you have told the truth? Veronica, please. If you don't, she'll kill both of us."

"And the power in that painting killed two men. Besides, how do I know I can trust you? You've lied to me this whole time."

"No one knows all my secrets. It's better that way."

"You speak like someone who hasn't been lied to their whole life."

Again, he got the sense there was something personal there. And if her talent for drawing had been locked away by some incident, what could he do?

"Why does she want the painting, anyway?" Veronica asked. "What does she want to do with it?"

"She thinks it will bring her eternal youth." Luc shook his head. "But it's not that simple."

"What isn't? I've seen what it can do to those whom it wants to harm. What else can it do?"

He felt the choice hanging between them. He could lie and make up something that would keep her away from his family secret, or he could tell her the truth. Could he trust her? He thought back to everything he'd seen of her and knew she'd be careful with the knowledge.

"It can confer a very long life. Not immortality—perhaps at one time it could, but the spell has weakened—but something akin to it. I'm a little over two hundred years old."

"Impossible." She put a hand to his unlined cheek. "You don't look more than a century."

"Ha ha." He caught her hand, but he appreciated her humor.

"And that's why my appearance pains me so. I'm stuck with it for at least another hundred." Phew, that hadn't been so bad. At least she hadn't stumbled upon—

"That's your real secret, isn't it?" She asked softly. "You're afraid that without your good looks, you won't have any power or influence, and you'll be doomed to a long, miserable life."

He couldn't speak. She'd just put his deepest fear into words.

"But your looks don't matter," she continued. "I've seen what you do, even with all your secrets. You're a good man, Luc."

"I'm a broken man, Veronica. But thank you."

Her hair rustled as she shook her head. "But two centuries? How is that possible?"

She'd just expressed faith in his goodness, and he wondered how she could accept that but doubt his age. Had his own perspective gotten so warped? "How, indeed? But how can a painting harbor a spirit?" And why had it not harmed her when she'd removed it from the chateau?

"And kill two men." She shivered, and he came to a conclusion he never would have expected. If the Legacy had harmed her, he would have destroyed it himself.

She continued in a small, frightened voice, "I always wondered if magic could be real. Now I wish it wasn't, although then I would never have met you."

"I gave up long ago on trying to figure out how things would be different if I hadn't inherited the Legacy. Too many mental pirouettes."

She laughed. "Now you sound like the Marquis I'd heard about." But her tone returned to somber. "I still don't know if I can draw the painting."

"Then we'll die together." He caught her to him. But their embrace didn't last long. The two pirates that had captured them flung the door open.

"The captain's ready to see you," the taller of the two snarled. "Both of you."

When Veronica imagined a pirate captain, she thought of a man with a beard and an eyepatch, not a slender blonde woman with green eyes and a sensual curve to her lips.

"Welcome to my ship, Mrs. Kindred," the captain—La Rouge—said. "I understand you threw something of mine away."

"It wasn't yours. Your people stole it." Veronica knew what she said would only make the situation worse. But she was tired of people trying to force her to do things, to control her actions and her future.

"Ah, but it was. Lautrec, show her what happens to people who take what is mine."

The burly pirate who had escorted Veronica to the captain put a knife to Luc's neck.

"I can carve him up right good, Miss. Or maybe take 'is other eye."

"No!" She held out her hands. "Fine. Yes, I threw the painting in the ocean, but I can recreate it." She swallowed, her hands shaking so hard she didn't know if she'd be able to put pencil to paper. "I can at least give you the important parts."

"Veronica, don't." Luc swallowed, and a drop of blood welled up where the motion of his neck muscles brought his skin into contact with the knife. She knew they didn't have much time. He didn't have much time. She couldn't allow him to be killed or spend the rest of his life—however many long years that could end up being—maimed more than he already was.

Don't waste your talents on him, the voice of doubt whispered in her brain. *He'll only betray you like your uncle. And Peter.*

Peter... He still haunted her. No, she *allowed* him to haunt her, his constant presence in her mind comfortable in its famil-iarity. That final conversation with him came back to her, his deathbed confession only a thought away.

"I knew your uncle had forbidden you to draw," he'd said. "And I had to go along with it while you were in school. I told you that you had no talent to protect you." He'd held out a hand, skeletal in its gauntness. "And me. If I'd nurtured your ability, you would have eventually chosen your art over me. I'm sorry."

She shoved the memory away, but the grief lingered. She'd lost the idea of who she'd thought her husband was, her faith in love, and her ability, which had been tied to betrayal from that moment on. It felt like she stood at the edge of a yawning precipice, her only options to fall backward into the known nothingness of losing it all again or to step forward and land where she may.

"Give me a piece of paper and a pencil," she said. "And allow me to sit at a writing surface."

The pirates complied, the captain watching her with a smile. Veronica wasn't stupid. She knew that she could as well have her throat slit and her body thrown overboard once she did what they asked. But that didn't matter at the moment, not if they had any chance of escape.

La Belle Rouge. She almost snorted and shook her head. What an ironic name for the airship and its captain. The pirate queen was beautiful externally, but the red of the blood of the people she'd killed or harmed stained her soul, and it wasn't pretty.

"We're waiting, Madame Kindred," Rouge said. "And I am growing impatient."

Right. Veronica took a long, shuddering breath and willed for her hand to move. She started with hesitant strokes, making the outline of the boy and his ball, forcing the details of the painting she'd spent so many hours staring at to come to mind.

Of course they did—she never forgot a piece of art. It was one reason Léonard, damn him, had made her his protégé.

The more she drew, the more the insistent voice that art would lead to betrayal waxed until she heard nothing except for its chant of *Stupid, Stupid, Stupid...*

Even if it does result in someone turning on me, in someone revealing a secret that could alter my life, I accept it. Her strokes grew more confident, the aspects of the painting springing to life beneath her hands as she sketched light and shadow. The child's eyes, although not in color, looked up at her with a wisdom beyond his years. A wisdom she now understood from Luc's strange and fascinating tale. *Even if disaster comes from this, it is worth it. I am worth it. This is me. This is me. This is me.*

The voice faded with her newly released confidence and the unadulterated joy of creation until all she could hear in her mind was, *This is me. I am an artist. I am worthy of my art.* She almost wept with the relief and the certainty that even in such a horrible situation, she could find her art and herself again. When she glanced up at Luc to make sure he was still all right, she saw him gazing at her with a sense of wonder. With a slight smile, she nodded and returned to the picture.

All that was left were the symbols on the ball. La Rouge leaned forward, her expression eager. "Yes, yes, that's it," she said. "Now the symbols."

Veronica put the pencil down and shook out her fingers. Her hand cramped from the years of not drawing, the muscles protesting the unfamiliar tension and motions. She also needed to think. She had been lied to, betrayed, and she hated it. Others' deception, regardless of their motives, had ruined her life, stealing the thing that made her happiest until this awful moment. Could she use her art to destroy rather than create? But what sort of creation would immortality for La Rouge look like? More killing and more blackmail. More lives made miserable. More injuries like Luc's.

"What are you doing?" La Rouge said. "Don't stop now, you stupid girl. Lautrec, the knife."

The man placed his bizarrely large hand around Luc's throat to hold him still and caressed Luc's undamaged cheek with the flat of the knife.

"Just taking a break," Veronica said lightly. "I'll get back to it in a moment."

"Fine. Don't take too long."

Veronica picked up the pencil. She remembered the symbols, the arcane squiggles that didn't mean anything to her but did to La Rouge and the others who understood such matters. Rather than recreate them exactly, she left one off and doubled another. She didn't know what that would do, but it felt right.

Was that why the spirit hadn't harmed her? Did it know she would come to this moment?

When she was finished, she handed the sketch to the captain. "There," she said. "You have it."

"*Bien*. Lautrec, lock him up in the hold. Formot, put her in there, too. I will prepare the ritual, and then they will see what rebirth into immortality looks like."

12

———

The pirate shoved Veronica into the dark holding cell, causing her to stumble. Luc caught her in his arms. She blinked to adjust her vision to the dim light provided by the one small porthole above them. It was near dark, and so the light had a velvet, purple quality. With the return of her artistic talent, the world had once again taken on a brightness of color and sharpness of line. She almost wept in gratitude, but one dark shadow remained. She'd betrayed her principles of honesty and integrity in order to keep La Rouge from attaining immortality. What would Luc think?

And then the certainty hit her that even if he hated her as a result, she wouldn't go back and do anything differently. But she could at least be honest in this moment.

"I am so proud of you," he murmured into her hair. "You did marvelously. And the sketch recreating the painting was perfect. Except..."

Oh, gods, he'd seen. He knew. But he hadn't said anything. If he had, it might have gotten her killed, so she could be grateful for that.

"I changed one of the symbols," she admitted. "I couldn't let that woman have immortality or even an extended Monceau-length lifespan. It wouldn't have been right. She's already hurt so many people, damaged so many lives." She buried her head in his chest. "But I understand if you think less of me for this. I broke my one life vow—I intentionally deceived."

He lifted her chin. "Do you think that in my long life I've ever met a perfectly honest person, Veronica? I have learned the hard way that circumstances sometimes require us to do things that are against our natures, to serve higher principles such as protecting others."

Her entire body loosened with relief and exhaustion, and he helped her to the narrow cot where they sat, their backs against the wall, and her head on his shoulder. She might have dozed but didn't know for how long when the door was thrown open, and Lautrec and Bonmot stood there along with Matthew, the ship's doctor who had betrayed them.

"It's time," the doctor said.

"For what?" Luc had his diffident nobleman voice on.

"For the ceremony. For La Belle Rouge to ascend to immortality. And if it works for her, she's promised to share it with me."

Veronica wanted to roll her eyes but dared not do anything so disrespectful in the presence of two large armed men who had the power to throw her overboard. The guards brought them to the deck, where an altar had been set up. The captain wore a long robe of white and had unbound her hair, and against the backdrop of the stars and bright moon, she looked like a pagan priestess. Veronica clutched Luc's hand and wished they knew what to expect.

Luc turned to her and whispered into her hair, "The escape compartments are at the back of the airship, two ladders down in the stern hatch. When the disaster strikes, go. I'll be right behind you."

Veronica nodded once, and he squeezed her hand. An electric tingling filled the air, and Veronica recognized it as a similar feeling to what had happened just before the painting had killed Firmin. It didn't help her feel better.

What collateral damage would the spirit of Monceau cause this time?

ON A SIGNAL LUC couldn't see, the pirates chanted something in a strange language. Luc tensed. He recognized it, not from having heard it, but from some long-distant ancestral memory. He'd studied Greek and knew the modern tongue, but this was an archaic dialect. Still, the meaning came across—petitioning the heavenly spheres to come into alignment to bless the ceremony. He shuddered when it appeared that the stars, at least some of them, moved, and he realized those were planets, not stars. Matthew tensed beside him, opposite Veronica.

"It's starting, can you feel it?" the ship's doctor asked, his tone gleeful. "La Belle Rouge will finally obtain what she deserves."

"Aye," Luc agreed, "what she deserves." Matthew looked at him sharply, but Luc shrugged. "You never know what may happen with these things." The weight of his ancestors and the spirit pressed in on him like it had at the chateau. He hoped that the change Veronica had made would be enough. Surely such rituals required precision?

Or would it backfire on all of them? Now he wished he'd studied more of the arcane arts that had interested his grandfather, the son of the Monceau who had made their Faustian bargain.

An aether isolation rig was brought forth, and with the help of the light reflected by the full moon, the aether appeared and stabilized. The little ouroboros in its glass globe undulated with the chanting. It grew brighter with each repetition, and soon Luc had to look away. The woman he'd known as Daphne Cinsault, who had been the person behind his misery for the past half year, placed her palms flat on the glass, and the chanting ceased. Now the absence of the thrumming of male voices heightened the hiss of the wind and the smell of the sea air.

Daphne chanted quietly, and she looked down at a piece of paper in front of her, her brow furrowed in concentration. The aether continued to move along with the sounds of her words, and Luc hoped that the ritual wouldn't work, prayed to whatever god may be listening that it wouldn't destroy him and Veronica should it turn on Daphne. He hadn't prayed in decades, having lost faith in whatever deity might be watching, and he'd even gone so far as to curse them after his injury, but now he made penance in his mind. And promised that if they got out of this, he'd complete what he'd started with opening himself up to Veronica. He'd told her his deepest secret, but he admitted he hadn't given her his heart although he knew they had developed feelings for each other. After seeing her bravely face down the pirates and confront her fear of what would happen if she were to draw, and then her adorable confession, how could he not?

He'd known plenty of women and had kept his entire self from all of them regardless of how much he admired them and what they did and said, so he could. But he wouldn't this time, and the breeze sighed around him as though his promise had been heard and understood.

The aether donut gradually warmed in shade turning yellow, then peach, then red, and then a sparkling black. Daphne broke off her chanting and laughed. Luc shivered at the sound, wondering what could be taking place in her spirit. Some sort of transformation? If the process delighted her so, they were all in trouble. But then her mirth died and turned into quiet sobs. Tears streamed down her face, and she tried to remove her hands from the glass, the muscles on her bare arms standing out with the effort, but she couldn't.

"Help me," she screamed. "You fools, help me. Smash the glass if you have to."

"No, you'll release whatever she's created," Luc said, but Lautrec and Matthew rushed forward and tried to pull her away. Lautrec removed his large dagger from its sheath, and with the hilt smashed the glass.

A roaring and rustling sound filled the air, the flight of a thousand desperate harpies. The dissonance thrummed through Luc, and he nudged Veronica. "Go!"

She nodded, lifted her skirts, and took off. He glanced back and saw the sparkling blackness expand, first engulfing Daphne and then Lautrec. He almost couldn't look away as it moved from pirate to pirate, all of whom had fled in whatever direction they could, and he shook himself out of his horrified stupor to follow Veronica. When he got to the hatch, he found Matthew there, blocking the way.

"You did that intentionally," the man spat. "You destroyed her. You stupid fucking nobleman—why couldn't you leave anything good for the rest of us?"

"What?" Luc asked, all too aware of the pressure behind him, the cold that preceded the roaring creature Daphne had created with Veronica's help. Another ancestral memory pushed forward—that it was a force of destruction born of a forced creation under mortal peril. The gods did not appreciate the gifts they'd given to humans being used for dark means, at least not the gods he wanted to worship.

"You created it, or your girl did." Matthew's face had gone red. "You can destroy it. If you do, I'll help you with Mrs. Kindred."

A chill that had nothing to do with the monster behind him spread through Luc's gut. Where had Veronica gone? "What did you do to her?"

"I only helped her down the stairs," Matthew said with a shrug. Luc looked down the hatch. In the dark, he could only make out a shape crumpled at the bottom. The gold accents on her clothes reflected the light, so he knew it was her.

"If I can't have love, you sure as hell can't," the other man growled.

Almost without thinking, Luc cocked a fist and punched Matthew in the nose. The doctor staggered back and then with a cry, fell backward over the railing. The roar of the creature drowned out his final yell and its abrupt end, although Luc couldn't help but imagine the sea swallowing him.

Luc descended the ladder into the hatch as quickly as he could and found Veronica unconscious but breathing. He looked up to see darkness covering the stars, and so with another prayer that he wouldn't accidentally make her injuries worse, he picked her up and dashed to the escape compartments. He arranged her as comfortably as he could, then closed the hatch and pulled the cord. A look out of the window showed him that darkness had overtaken the entire La Belle Rouge. He watched, unable to look away, as it engulfed the ship, then folded in on itself and grew so small as to wink out of existence.

The wooden box that made up the bottom of the escape compartment swung slightly under the parachutes. He hoped they would float when they hit the water.

"Luc?" Veronica asked, blinking sleepily. "What happened?" She scooted to a sitting position. "And where am I?"

"We escaped." For the first time in almost a century, he allowed himself to laugh, a true belly laugh. "We escaped."

13

———

A buzzing sound alerted Luc to the strange sight of a winged creature following them. The moonlight shone silver on it, and it had a head sticking up in the middle of it. No, that wasn't the creature's head—it belonged to a man with goggles.

"It's Inspector Davidson," said Veronica. "What is that thing?"

"It looks like some sort of steam machine," Luc replied. When it got closer, he recognized the man's sandy brown hair and determined jawline.

"Marquis! Mrs. Kindred," Davidson called. "I'm going to hook you and try to direct you back to the *Acadia Pearl*."

Davidson swung around in his strange craft, and something caught with a thunk on the outside of the compartment, which tilted. Luc caught Veronica, and she grinned up at him. He smiled back at her even though it hurt, although not as much as previously.

"You look like you're enjoying this," he said.

"Incredibly." She looked outside. "I never would have

thought when I left the States that I'd have such adventures. But what happened to La Belle Rouge?"

Luc shuddered. "The spirit took its revenge. I don't know what she awakened, but it was angry."

She ran her fingers through the hair at his temple. "Your sides have gone gray."

Whereas such words would have previously horrified him, he now bowed his head under what it did—could—mean. "Then the spirit—and the Legacy—of Monceau have left me. I'll age like a mortal man now." Emotions flooded through him, but he couldn't catch one long enough to stick with it. Relief that he hadn't immediately turned into a corpse. Regret that he hadn't used his previous longevity better. Sadness that part of him—as much as he'd cursed it—was gone. Anxiety that his eye would never grow back now. And then hope. Hope that he would be able to grow old with someone, not watch her age and die. Hope that he'd be supported in his inevitable grief. And joy that he wouldn't curse his children with the double-edged sword that a centuries-long life could be.

Speaking of which, if he wanted to follow through on his intentions, he had to make sure. After all the women he'd known, he'd never had one he cared so much about. And so he had to tread carefully. He didn't care if he sounded like a gentleman from a previous century. It was time he started acting like one.

"Mrs. Kindred—may I call you Veronica? I know I have, but I haven't asked."

She laughed. "Yes, I believe you can. We've been through enough together. What shall I call you?"

"I believe Luc will do. I have another question for you."

She tilted her face up to him, her golden eyes inquisitive. "Yes?"

"May I court you?"

She laughed. "Yes, Marquis—Luc—you may."

WHEN VERONICA KNOCKED on the door of Theresa Kindred's house on the Battery in Charleston, she didn't know what to expect. Peter had been tall, so she couldn't imagine he had come from the petite woman who answered the door and looked up at her. The sounds of construction, the rebuilding of the city after its siege, surrounded them, but Veronica had no trouble picking out Theresa's words.

"Oh, you must be Veronica! Why, Peter said you were pretty but didn't say you were a work of art."

Veronica looked down at her clothing, which she'd thought appropriately somber for the visit, but Luc's influence showed. He'd helped her pick out a dark purple jacket and skirt over a blouse of cream silk and vest of mauve. Her hat matched the rest of her outfit and sported black feathers and jet beads.

"Thank you," was the only thing Veronica could think of to say to the ball of energy who'd been Peter's mother. Theresa pulled her inside.

"He spoke often of you while he was here. He tried to get me to go back to Terminus with him, but I couldn't leave my home."

Veronica nodded. So Theresa was as stubborn as her son. "You were lucky, then."

"Yes, we were spared the worst of it. I think the Yankees wanted to preserve this section so they could take it over. Tea?"

Theresa prattled on. Veronica got the sense she hadn't had much chance to talk to someone about Peter. Veronica decided five minutes into the conversation that she wouldn't tell her late husband's mother that her beloved son Peter had conspired with Veronica's uncle to stifle her talent. It didn't matter now. She had her drawing again, and she once again believed in love, even though that had come more slowly.

When the visit ended, Theresa pulled Veronica into an

embrace. "I'm so glad you stopped by. Peter's brother would have loved to have met you, but he's out and about on business today."

"That's fine. Please tell him I'm sorry I missed him." She didn't promise to return, and Theresa didn't insist that she did. With a sad smile, Theresa walked Veronica to the door, but then turned.

"My dear girl, I know my sons. And I know that Peter sometimes did stupid things because he thought he knew what was best for everyone but himself. He got that from me. Whatever he did to you, please forgive him. He never meant to hurt you."

"Thank you." Veronica blinked so the tears wouldn't start. She hadn't realized it, but she wanted an apology from him, and this was the closest she'd get. She nodded and again said, "Thank you."

When she walked outside, the day seemed brighter, and she smiled to see Luc waiting for her in a carriage.

"Right on time, *ma cherie*," he said. He, too, wore purple. "Where shall we have dinner? Let's celebrate this last night here."

Veronica allowed him to pull her into the whirlwind of his true personality, which sometimes overwhelmed her, but which she couldn't help but adore. How could she not? His unapologetic genuineness charmed her a hundred times per day, as did his consideration. And then on the morrow, they'd be on their way to Terminus.

As the carriage pulled Veronica away from Theresa Kindred's house and that part of her past, she thought about what her uncle would say when she showed up with a pirate. But he could no longer control her future, and she didn't fear him.

Whatever happened, she had her art, and she'd not allow herself to lose it again.

The End

Thank you for reading The Art of Piracy! I hope you enjoyed reading about Veronica and Luc as much as I loved writing them. Veronica, being an artist, turned into one of my favorite characters, and of course I always wanted to know more about the mysterious Marquis from the Aether Psychics books.

Reviews are so very helpful for us authors, both to let us know what you want more and less of, and to help other readers find our books. Please consider leaving an honest review on Goodreads and the site where you bought the book. I'd really appreciate it!

ABOUT MISSION: NUTCRACKER

Continue the *Inspector Davidson Mysteries* series with *Mission: Nutcracker*.

She dreams of joining the scientific elite. He's desperate to save his business and his sister. Together, they may hold the turnkey to adventure...

Terminus, 1871. Fiona Telfair won't give up her gears and gadgets for the ball and chain of marriage. But her future as a tinkerer comes under attack when nutcracker automatons raid the trade hall masquerade party and kidnap her fellow inventors. With her brilliant engineer father among those taken, Fiona's only hope of rescuing him lies with the captivating rail baron who rescued her from the fray.

Devon Meriweather can only keep his train empire on track if he marries into an influential family. And he also needs the connections to make sure his chronically ill sibling can marry well. So no matter how engaging and beautiful the firmly working-class Fiona may be, he knows she'll only ever be a partner in solving crimes.

As they work closely hunting for clues to the strange

aether-powered apparatus and magical mice, the intrepid duo can't deny their budding feelings. But neither can afford a distracting courtship with the growing threat of the nutcrackers and their deadly chompers.

Can Fiona and Devon expose the menacing mastermind behind the machines and make their passion run like clockwork?

Mission: Nutcracker is the second book in the charming Inspector Davidson Mysteries steampunk romance series. If you like plucky heroines, nineteenth-century mystique, and unusual Christmas fairytale retellings, then you'll love Cecilia Dominic's yuletide triumph.

Buy Mission: Nutcracker and steam headlong into holiday fun today!

For more information, go to:
ceciliadominic.com/mission-nutcracker

To grab your copy of Mission: Nutcracker, go to:
Books2read.com/mission-nutcracker

Or order it from Ingram Spark through your favorite physical bookstore with the following ISBN: 978-1-945074-51-6

Please keep reading to check out the first chapter of *Mission: Nutcracker*

MISSION: NUTCRACKER PREVIEW

erminus, 16 December 1871

Fiona pulled on her old gloves, which were already dingy but now made more so by a liberal application of coal dust. She smeared some of the dark gray matter on her cheeks, distributing it so it would draw the viewer's gaze to her sparkling blue eyes. Her mask and headpiece with round ears in place, she stepped back from the mirror to check out her costume. Yes, in spite of the mask having a pointed nose with ridiculous whiskers, she made quite the fetching mouse. And the best part—the costume, which consisted of a simple gray dress she'd worn as part of her half-mourning—had been made of salvaged clothing and parts. She hadn't spent any of the money set aside for her upcoming debut season, so her mother couldn't argue with her desire or right to go to the Tinkerer's Holiday Masquerade Ball.

Well, not unless she found out Fiona had been one of the few unattached females invited. But she didn't need to know that. Fiona trusted her father not to tell, although he'd been known to slip.

A knock on the door startled her out of her thoughts, which

had started to creep toward old, familiar territory. How could her brother have gotten himself killed and left her alone to manage her mother? Connor had been her mother's favorite child. Fiona had never measured up.

"Are you ready, Pet?"

Fiona smiled at her father's voice. "Yes, Papa. Be right out."

She gave herself one more look from the front, and then another from the back. Good, her dress showed off her small waist and the white skin of her neck, and the dim light would keep anyone from noticing the freckles that popped out no matter what she did to get rid of them. Her dark red hair would shine like burnished copper in the candlelight, and what better to attract a handsome young inventor than copper? And her mind, which several of the tinkerers had said they admired. Granted, they hadn't been *looking* at her mind at the time, but they shifted their gazes upward when they started discussing aether theory...

Another knock brought her back to herself. Then her father's voice. "The steamcart is here."

Again, her thoughts had run away with her. Her father laughed when that happened. Her mother sniffed disapprovingly.

"There's nothing wrong with a girl with a quick mind," her father would say.

"Not unless it keeps her from catching a rich husband." *Sniff.* The sound made Fiona cringe every time. It even followed her into her dreams. Ever since Connor had died, that had become her mother's refrain—catch a rich husband. Maybe then Fiona would finally earn her approval.

Well, Fiona was on the hunt tonight, but for brains, not money. She had faith that the latter would come from the former. Education could be bought. Intelligence could not.

Fiona walked out of her bedroom to find her father hilariously dressed as a cat. His gray mask had black tabby stripes painted on it, and he'd used kohl to continue the stripes on the side of his face. He'd even fixed pointed ears into his curly gray-specked black hair. His bright blue eyes—the same as Fiona's—twinkled behind the mask. Otherwise, he wore all black evening dress with an emerald pin—his one piece left from his Irish father—in his cravat.

He kissed her cheek. "You look lovely, Miss Mouse."

She giggled. "And you look ridiculous, Professor Cat."

"That's my job, Pet. To bring attention to the belle of the ball. And I have something for you." He brought out a small box and gave it to her. Inside, nestled in cotton fluff, lay a dark gray chain with a pendant shaped like something that looked like a cross between a walnut and a macadamia nut.

"What is it?" Fiona asked. "And what is the material?"

"A krakatuk nut locket. It's an old family heirloom, and I don't know about the metal. Your mother wanted me to wait until Christmas, but I thought I should give it to you now. Why don't you hide it in your room so she doesn't know?"

"Thank you. It's lovely." Fiona took one last look at it and stuck it in the drawer of her dressing table.

They descended the stairs of their modest townhouse. Fiona's mother waited at the bottom.

Sniff. "Well, you're a fine pair." She crossed her arms over the black mourning dress she still wore. Her perpetual frown had drawn lines beside her lips, but otherwise she looked like an older, heavier version of Fiona. "Don't be out too late."

"Yes, Mother."

Fiona's father kissed his wife on the cheek, and Fiona smirked to see a little of the coal dust had rubbed on to him, and therefore on to her mother. Or maybe he'd smudged a stripe.

"I'll have her back before midnight. It would be awkward for her to turn into a pumpkin, after all."

Another sniff and not the faintest hint of a smile, although

Fiona grinned at his joke. She'd thought about dressing as a pumpkin, but she didn't have anything orange, as it was not a flattering color on her.

They almost ran out of the door and into the steamcart. Had this been a ball at one of the fine houses, they might have rented a carriage with real horses. But mechanical conveyance fit this particular party.

Once he'd confirmed Fiona was comfortable, her father lapsed into silence. He gazed out of the window, his hairline tight above his mask and his lips pursed below it, so she didn't disturb him. Instead, she followed her own mental meanderings. One more check of the contents of her reticule, then back to the mathematical problem she'd been attempting to solve all week.

When the steamcart drew up to the door, Fiona's father paid the driver and instructed him to return at eleven-thirty. The Tinkerer's Guild Hall had been decorated in reds and greens. No religious imagery—they tended to shy away from objects that would remind the members of the long war they'd just come through and the losses they'd each experienced. No one wanted to think of funerals or discord as they all struggled to make sense of their new world.

Fiona and her father walked through the ballroom and nodded to acquaintances they recognized. Some wore costumes that covered their heads and all or part of their faces, making it more difficult for Fiona to identify them. The costumes ranged from scientific concepts and tools to animals or characters. One commonality—they all wore a concerned expression that would appear between words and smiles, reminding Fiona that some of their number had been disappearing. Indeed, the ball seemed less crowded than she'd expected. But at least they were all safe here among their own kind, weren't they?

"Oh, there's Thaddeus." Fiona's father veered to the right

toward an older gentleman who, along with Fiona's father, was a Master Tinkerer. "Will you be all right on your own for a bit? I have some things I need to ask him."

"Yes, Papa. I'm going to get some punch."

His smile gave him the look of a mischievous cat. "Don't drink too much. Some young buck always adds spirits to it before the night is over."

"Yes, Papa." She wandered around the periphery of the ballroom. A chamber group played on a small stage between decorated trees, which held flickering candles and strings of popcorn. The gas sconces along the wall provided dim light. During meetings, the flames would be turned to medium or high so the members could see the books and papers being discussed, but tonight the lamps gave the room a warm, lovely glow. Fiona smiled—no seeing her freckles here! Some people danced, but tinkerers preferred to talk—well, argue—hence the limited number of musicians.

The sparkling of cut glass cups and a ladle in a stand beside a large crystal bowl drew her attention to the punch table. As she moved closer, the apple and cherry smells of the pinkish liquid made her mouth water. Ah, yes, the famed Tinkerer Hall punch, only served once a year at the holiday ball. Who had lent the family crystal to the party?

"May I pour you some punch?" The man's deep voice resonated through her, and Fiona turned and stifled a gasp. Of course Devon Meriweather hadn't bothered with any sort of costume, merely a plain black mask over the top half of his face. Still, she'd recognize him anywhere.

Fiona opened her mouth to speak, but only a squeak came out. Surely her face must be turning red beneath her mask.

"Ah, I admire your staying in character." He grinned and picked up a cup and the ladle. "I'll take that as a yes."

She nodded. For some reason she could converse comfortably with any of the other young men who had returned after the war ended, but she couldn't string more than a few words together for the handsome but arrogant Meriweather.

He handed her the punch, and she did manage a, "Thank you."

"You're very welcome. Have you read anything good lately?"

Fiona hid her jaw drop by sipping the punch. No heat to indicate it had been tampered with—yet. She'd mentioned once that she liked Edgar Allan Poe—one of her few moderately successful and brief conversations with Meriweather—but he'd teased her about her morbid tastes.

She shook her head and took another sip, the words she wanted fleeing her brain like, well, mice before a cat.

"Ah, too bad. I've twisted my ankle and have been laid up, so I've been seeking recommendations."

"Is that why you're not dancing?" she blurted. *Right, go for the inappropriate, almost personal question.* She didn't even know if he danced.

"Well, that and I hadn't yet found a partner who interested me enough to give it a try." He sipped his own punch, but the look he gave her over the glass made her cheeks heat again. Was he asking her to dance? What if he was? If it was hard to talk to him, how much worse would it be to dance?

Why didn't he leave her alone?

The questions flew so fast through her brain she tried to swallow and breathe at the same time, and she went into a coughing fit. He guided her hand to put her cup down. "Here, let me find you some water."

She nodded and tried to melt into the shadows, as her coughing had attracted the curious and concerned looks of the people around her. Coils, what had been in that punch?

When she finally got her breath back without any help from Meriweather, who had disappeared, Fiona took a couple of sips from her punch glass, which had stayed where she left it. People had returned to their conversations—thank goodness.

But then the murmuring faded to whispers. The small hairs on her arms raised, and the temperature in the room dropped as the shadows along the edge deepened. She found the source of the disturbance—someone had come dressed as the Masque of the Red Death. They strode to the center of the room.

Fiona took in the physique of the person. Tall, thin, with dark wavy hair—or at least, so she thought. Why did it relieve her that the person looked too gaunt to be Devon?

Her father rushed to her side. "Fiona, we have to go. Now."

She didn't argue, but when they turned toward the exit and joined the flow of the crowd, who had been edging toward the door, automatons clanged through the one entrance. They looked like giant German nutcracker dolls with white breeches and red jackets. But not benign ones—their eyes glowed over their painted-on rictus grins.

Curses from the men and shrieks from the women joined the roar of fire as the sconces on the walls turned sideways and shot flames out of both sides. Curtains, picture frames, and anything else flammable moved from smoldering to burning in mere seconds, and smoke joined the darkness in the air. Now Fiona coughed again.

Fiona's father tugged on her arm. "This way." He pulled her behind the punch table and pressed on a section of molding. Part of the wall folded inward. "Secret entrance for servants to replenish the refreshments without being seen," he explained. "We can get out through the back."

"Fiona! And Bryan. Thank God you have her." Devon Meriweather appeared followed closely by his doppelganger. No, his cousin Pierce, whom Fiona had only met once. If possible, he was even more arrogant than Devon.

"I need to find Thaddeus and Hollowell," Fiona's father said. "Can you get her out of here?"

"Yes. Let's go." Devon placed Fiona's hand on his arm, and they ducked into the passage and descended a staircase. Light shone at the end of it—the kitchens, which were in a state of panic as servants had managed to escape from the ballroom and tell the others what had started to happen.

"Everyone, get out." Devon didn't need to shout—his voice carried enough for people to hear him. "The hall is on fire. Where's the way out?"

"This way, Sir." One of the waiters who had been carrying champagne through the ballroom gestured for Devon to follow, and Fiona was swept along with him. She kept looking back for her father.

Once outside, they met up with a group of partygoers. They huddled at the far end of the lawn in a copse of trees, where they could observe but not be seen too easily. Or maybe their curiosity overcame their senses of preservation—tinkerers could be like that.

Fiona pulled away from Devon and joined her friends Lucy and Posey Lillet, who, fortunately this time, arrived late for everything.

"Fiona, are you all right? Were you in the fire?" one woman asked. Fiona recognized Lucy's mother. A pang of jealousy joined Fiona's anxiety. What must it be like to have a mother who supported her daughter's dreams?

Right, she had coal on her face. "No, I'm fine. Where is everyone? Did they get out?"

"Maybe." Fiona's anxiety flared like the fire when the woman gestured upward.

Orange and yellow flames illuminated the black balloon and gondola of the airship that hovered over the roof. Fiona could barely make out automatons, which shone with reflected flickering, herding darker shapes on to a gangplank that led inside. Then they, too, disappeared, and the vehicle took off, almost mocking in its slowness. It faded into the night sky.

The fire brigade had arrived and attempted to douse the flames, but soon it became apparent that all they could do was keep it from spreading. The strength left Fiona's legs, and she leaned against Devon.

Where was her father? Had he been taken in the airship? A certain sense—the same one that indicated to Fiona when she was close to the answer of a stubborn problem—told her yes.

She had to find him before they hurt him, but how? And why hadn't she insisted he come with her? Dread joined the fear that tightened her chest—she'd have to manage her mother before she could do anything else.

Want to see what happens next in Mission: Nutcracker? Go to:
Books2read.com/mission-nutcracker

Or order it from Ingram Spark through your favorite physical bookstore!

ABOUT THE AUTHOR

By day, clinical psychologist Cecilia Dominic helps people cure their insomnia. By night, this urban fantasy and steampunk author writes fiction that keeps her readers turning pages past bedtime. She prefers the term "versatile" to "conflicted" and has published both short story and novel-length fiction. She lives in Atlanta, Georgia, with her husband and the world's cutest cat.

You can find out more about her and her books at her website:

ceciliadominic.com

Sign up for Cecilia's newsletter and get a steampunk novella at the following link:

https://www.
subscribepage.com/CeciliaDominicbackofbook

I hate spam and promise to keep your email safe!

facebook.com/CeciliaDominicAuthor

twitter.com/ceciliadominic

instagram.com/randomoenophile

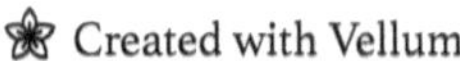 Created with Vellum

9 781945 074523